COMES

—Patrick D'Orazio—

THE DARK

Comes the Dark
By Patrick D'Orazio
Copyright 2010. All Rights reserved

ISBN10 - 1453701281
ISBN13 - 9781453701287

Edited by Michelle Linhart
Cover art by Phillip Rogers
Interior formatting by Kody Boye

To my wife, Sheli, who always believed in me, and to my kids, Ali and Zack, who share my sense of awe and wonder at the worlds we can create within our minds and then put down on a piece of paper. I love you all.

INTRODUCTION

What would you do if your entire world crumbled before your eyes and every one you ever loved was ripped from you?

If someone asked me to describe this book and its two sequels, I think that question would probably be as good a starting point as any. This book is a tale of normal, everyday people trying to come to grips with the horrors of a world where everything they have ever known has been wiped out.

That's what I wanted to create when I came up with the idea for *Comes the Dark*. From its inception, it was a story about an average guy, Jeff Blaine, coming to grips with the destruction of his world. And it's not just about survival; it's about finding a *reason* to survive. For Jeff, it's about getting revenge on the monsters that destroyed his wife and children. For the others he meets, it's about hope or perhaps an attempt to retain a tenuous grasp on a life not filled with nightmares. And as these survivors journey deeper into the darkness of their new world, they start to realize they have another question to answer: *what are you willing to do to survive?*

This is also a story of the undead apocalypse. Zombies play a major role in this story and they play their part well. Zombies, unlike other monster archetypes, are not the main characters in most stories they inhabit. They allow the human race to seal its own fate, whether on a grand scale or down to the individual level. Unlike vampires, werewolves, and other supernatural beings, they don't necessarily like the spotlight, but when they are in it, they tend to share it with a cast of thousands of their own kind. Their greatest strength, in my humble opinion, is that they have a knack for providing the catalyst necessary to allow humans to be ... human.

No book is written in a vacuum. As such, there are far too many people for me to thank for making this book possible. From its birth as an idea back in 2006 to the day the Library of the Living Dead released it in 2010, there have been those people who provided me with encouragement, advice, and critiques that made me keep going back to the drawing board until I got it right...or as close to right as I could get it. So I would like to try and do my best to thank the folks who loaned me their ears, provided me with insights, advice, and brutal honesty. Your efforts have not gone unnoticed. If I miss anyone, please forgive me-there are far too many people out there who made this possible and as I age, my memory continues to slip, so I will use that as my feeble excuse. So with that in mind, I would like to thank David Ravitch, Mike Olsson, Rob Cima, Steve Vonderhaar, Joe Roman, John Boehm, Amy LaRoche, Steve North, Tim Long, David Dunwoody, Ben Rogers, Kim Paffenroth, Lee Hartnup, Michelle Linhart, Philip Rogers, Dr. Pus, and the rest of the folks at the Library of the Living Dead who have offered encouragement, support, and enthusiasm for all things zombie. I also want to thank my mom and dad for giving me the desire to not only read and create, but to have a passion for learning that continues to this day. I have left the most important people for last and the most deserving of my gratitude: my wife, Sheli, and my children, Ali and Zack, who have supported me and believed in me from the instant I proclaimed that I wanted to write a novel. Heck, that isn't even fair. I want to thank them for giving me the encouragement to do this long before I ever started writing, and believing that I always had it in me to create something. For that, they have my undying love and gratitude.

The sun's rim dips;
the stars rush out:
At one stride comes the dark.

From "The Rime of the Ancient Mariner" by Samuel Taylor Coleridge

Chapter 1

Jeff bit his lip as he tried to maintain a grip on the aluminum baseball bat in his sweaty hands. He splashed through a slick puddle of blood as he continued running down the sidewalk.

The backpack jounced up and down and he slipped his hand around the strap to make sure it stayed in place. The tin cans and boxes of crackers thumped in time to his footsteps. Increasing his speed, he tried to suck in another lungful of air.

The howls of rage had grown distant but slowing down wasn't an option. Not until he was safely back inside. As he crested the hill a smile tugged at Jeff's lips—there were only a few more houses to pass and he would be home free.

Pulling tighter on the frayed strap hanging over his shoulder, he moved onto the grass to avoid hearing his own footsteps. Eyes darting back and forth, he spied no movement as his house came into view. It was hard to believe it had only been an hour since he had crept out to go on a hunt for food. He spotted the dark brown side door, which stood in stark contrast to the light beige siding that surrounded it.

Skidding to a halt in front of the door, Jeff's eyes

narrowed. There was a smudge near the knob. A rusty red finger-shaped outline caused his heart to skip a beat.

Feeling a rush of white hot terror flooding his system, Jeff looked around, eyes shifting to the bushes at the back of his neighbor's house. He could feel his heart racing and pulse accelerate as he tried to keep his breathing normal. Turning quickly, he looked across the street at the other houses, scanning for movement among the shadows. Ignoring the moans and howls off in the distance, he tried to reassure himself no one was watching or waiting to pounce. Taking a deep breath, he tried to tell himself that everything was going to be okay.

The smudge had not been there before. He recalled staring at the door after shutting it earlier and wondering if leaving, even if for a little while, was such a good idea. There had been no scratches and certainly no blood on the door when he left. That was not something the detail oriented man would have missed.

Jeff dug into his pocket and curled his fingers around the house key. Regardless of whoever...*or whatever*...had left the mark on the door all that mattered now was getting back inside before he was discovered out here.

As the key touched the knob and the door moved slightly, Jeff's eyes widened and his hand began to quiver. The door was already unlocked. Worse, it wasn't even shut. He began to shake his head and whisper *"no"* over and over. It couldn't be.

Jeff *knew* he had locked the door when he left. He had hugged Ellen, told Frankie and Mary to behave for mommy, and then...

A cold, stark fear for his family's safety overrode the slow itch of terror in Jeff's gut as he slammed his fist into the door and burst into the garage. Staring into the darkened space, he nearly stumbled but somehow his watery legs managed to hold him up.

Mark, his next door neighbor, was bent over Ellen, teeth buried in her neck. A wide pool of bright red fluid gushed from where he gnawed at her torn flesh.

Jeff froze in the doorway as he desperately tried to comprehend what he was seeing. The guy he had shared a few beers with over discussions about politics, baseball, and the Horton's Rottweiler crapping in their yards was tearing into his wife's throat. Jeff couldn't quite see Ellen's face because Mark's blood-drenched hand was clasped over her eyes and nose, but it was definitely her. There was a faint scent of jasmine in the air mixed in with the rich coppery scent of blood. It was that perfume she always wore. The tenth anniversary diamond ring he had given her a year before sparkled in a splash of sunlight as her arm flopped to the side. Jeff's eyes gravitated to the ring but it was hard to catch more than a brief glimpse of it as his wife's fingers twitched violently in response to the tearing motion of Mark's teeth.

The door, already forgotten, banged against the wall. Jeff did not hear the sound over the pounding of his heart but Mark did. The grayish figure lifted his head and hissed at Jeff, his teeth caked with bits of Ellen's flesh. Ragged runners of gruel bubbled from his mouth as the lunatic huddled protectively over his prize.

All Jeff could think was that this was madness. In a few seconds Mark would wink at him and Ellen would sit up and say something like "gotcha." Then they would all laugh at how gullible Jeff had been to even believe for a second that any of this was real.

But as waves of horror washed over him, Jeff tried and failed to deny the reality of what he was seeing. Mark's milky white eyes peered up at him; dark pinpricks that had been his pupils the only color remaining in them. Forcing himself to look away from the crumpled form of his wife, Jeff stared at his neighbor once again. Mark's shirt was torn open and hung slack on his oddly colored flesh. There were various sores and open wounds displayed on his neck, arms, and chest. Greenish-black ooze stained the infected man's clothing and as he began to lever his body up, the stench slammed into Jeff like a sledgehammer.

Jeff wanted to run. He wanted to run screaming from this place and never look back. But as he shifted his gaze back to the only woman he had ever loved, a hundred different memories flooded into his mind, blotting out the image of the gore-stained lump of flesh that remained behind: kissing her for the first time at midnight on New Year's Eve...burning the dinner he had cooked for her on the night he proposed...watching her and Mary drench the kitchen in flour when they tried to bake cookies together. There was an echoing scream rattling inside Jeff's head but he couldn't get it past his lips. All those memories, along with his wife, had been obliterated in the blink of an eye.

Jeff tried to take a step back but discovered his shoulder was pressed against the doorjamb, blocking his escape. His legs had moved of their own volition, dragging the stunned survivor backwards until there was nowhere left to go. As Mark finally rose up and moved slowly toward him, Jeff realized he couldn't breathe anymore.

Mark's eyes fixed on Jeff and he felt his legs and arms stiffen in terror. The lunatic's pupils were almost hypnotic as they burrowed into him. There was great pain and rage in those eyes, but more than anything, there was hunger...a profound hunger that could devour the world if given the chance.

As the ghoul dragged its ruined body over Ellen's corpse it tripped and staggered. Jeff blinked as he watched the bogeyman right himself awkwardly. In that moment, it was as if the world suddenly snapped back into place. Mark had turned into some kind of monster to be feared, that much was true, but he was also the bastard that had murdered his wife. Watching carefully as Mark pulled his back foot over Ellen's prone form, Jeff gripped the baseball bat tightly as he got into a wobbly batter's stance.

The swing was not his best but it still connected with Mark's arm, sending him sideways. There was a muffled thump as the bat connected with the infected man's spoiled flesh. Jeff's eyes widened when Mark did not react to the painful blow, his milky-white eyes never losing sight of their target. Adjusting, Mark got his feet back underneath him and kept coming.

The second swing was stronger, aimed at Mark's face. It connected with the ghoul's neck instead and there was an audible crack as bones broke. Mark's head twisted, wrapping around the bat as his skin stretched and tore. His knees buckled but he did not fall over immediately. Instead, one of his arms shot out in an effort to grab a hold of Jeff's shirt.

Letting go of the bat, Jeff pushed back against the wall even harder, doing his best to burrow through the drywall. The bat clattered to the floor and Mark took a single wavering step forward before collapsing. His head slammed into the concrete with an audible thud.

Jeff stood stiffly next to the slumped over body for what seemed an eternity. He stared into his neighbor's eyes as a torrent of emotions poured over him. Irrationally, he feared the repercussions of murdering his neighbor though Mark would probably argue that he wasn't dead if he could still speak. Instead, the ghastly creature stared balefully up at Jeff as small noises burbled from his shattered throat. Unable to move his body, Mark continued to grind his teeth and hiss, unchecked rage carved on his face.

When Jeff's heart rate settled and he started to breathe normally he unglued his eyes from the man at his feet and looked at his wife, whose appendages were no longer twitching. Crumpled, with legs bunched up underneath her, Jeff could see the rubber burn marks on the floor beneath her beat up sneakers. It was clear she had struggled fiercely, even as Mark sunk his teeth into her throat. *She was always a fighter*, he thought. Now that Ellen's face was no longer covered Jeff could see that her eyes weren't shut, a look of terror still on her face. There was agony in those green eyes...an agony that must have been the last thing she had felt.

Jeff's knees gave way and he crumpled to the ground. Slamming his eyes shut he willed the horrible images of

Ellen's death that were burned into his retinas to go away. He felt dizzy and nauseous but since he had not eaten in nearly a day there would probably be nothing but dry heaves when the sickness finally overpowered him.

That was when he heard a blood curdling scream from down the street.

It had taken every last bit of his willpower to not curl up in a ball when he heard the noises coming from less than a block away. They had tracked him down. By the time he levered himself up from the floor and moved past Mark to slam and lock the door, he could hear them getting closer. His neighbors were closing in on the house. Jeff didn't have the strength to look outside and see how many there were. Instead, he leaned against the door, panting and exhausted as the moans grew louder.

Raising his head, his eyes suddenly darted around and his body tensed. He tried to blot out the noises outside so he could capture another sound just hitting his ears. He looked at the door leading into the house.

Adrenaline flooded Jeff's system again as reality came crashing down. The sound coming through the door was clearer than the muffled roars of anger and hunger bellowing from outside and yet...it sounded very familiar.

He began to hyperventilate, shaking his head in disbelief. How could he have been so stupid? How could he have blanked out and forgotten?

But the blood splatters in the laundry room confirmed what the cold, calculating part of Jeff's brain already understood but the rest of him refused to believe.

Mark wasn't the only one that had gotten into the house.

Jeff flew through the door. Everything inside him screamed that he had to move quickly, get inside, and stop these marauders. But as he heard the moans coming from upstairs he feared he was already too late.

Jeff steeled himself as he rushed inside; hoping against hope that he was wrong, and that somehow these monsters that had once been human had not found his children's hiding place upstairs.

A short time later Jeff returned to the garage, his eyes dull, his arms splattered with blood. The aluminum bat was slung over his shoulder, dripping a thick, tar-like substance.

He ignored the pounding and screams of rage outside the garage door. They had found him, after all this time. The insanity outside had finally broken into his home and annihilated everything he knew.

As he slumped to the wooden steps, the small window on the side door shattered and was quickly followed by the sound of fists thumping on the thick slab of wood nailed behind it. Jeff idly wondered how long his jury-rigged barricade would hold up and if it really mattered anymore. He set the bat down and put his chin in his hands, propping his elbows on his knees.

As he sat listening to the scratching and clawing, interspersed with ragged fists splattering against the wood, he glanced down at the two bodies in the garage. He took a deep breath into his lungs, doing his best to ignore the thick taste of death that came with it. Mark was facing away so at least the man wasn't staring at him.

His eyes slid from Mark to the pile of gas cans in the corner. Several propane tanks sat next to the smaller canisters, along with some other odds and ends Jeff had picked up a few weeks back when things had started getting dicey. He shook his head in disbelief. Back then their worst concern was potential power outages and being forced to use the barbeque grill for all their cooking.

His eyes left the pile of supplies and moved back toward his wife. Jeff wondered when he was going to cry. His eyes were still dry, even as he looked at the ragged blood filled hole Mark had left where her throat had been. He hadn't cried inside the house, even as he cradled his dead daughter and whispered her name over and over again.

The pounding outside was getting louder. It sounded like there was an army of them out there. They hadn't moved to the front yard yet, but it wouldn't be long. Then it was only a matter of time before they tore through the hastily nailed up boards and plywood covering the windows and found their way inside.

Twisting his neck around to loosen up the stiffness, Jeff stood up. Gazing down on his wife, he recalled how her eyes used to sparkle like a thousand tiny emeralds. That green was gone now, replaced with the telltale cloudiness that warned of infection.

When her hand twitched Jeff backpedaled, slipping on the stairs and falling hard on his ass. Slowly, he felt his body grow cold as it became clear what was happening. Head slumping in defeat, he rubbed his eyes and knew what he had to do.

Her hand twitched again. Ellen was waking up.

Grabbing for his bat, Jeff cradled it to his chest. His hands felt weak and useless, but he held on to the aluminum cylinder like a security blanket.

Suddenly, a sound like someone ramming their head against the side door made him jump. Looking over, he saw that the wood was starting to splinter.

Spying Mark out of the corner of his eye, Jeff saw that despite a broken neck, his neighbor had managed to shift his head enough so he could stare at Jeff again. The hunger in those eyes was undeniable and Jeff knew he couldn't bare it if he had to see that same look in Ellen's eyes.

Taking another deep breath, he stood and lifted the baseball bat. The fear was gone, replaced with a depthless despair. His wife's legs were starting to move. Her eyes were still vacant and empty, but wouldn't be for long.

"I love you honey," Jeff choked out as he felt the strength return to his hands. He gripped the bat tighter and raised it above his head.

The first swing took every ounce of courage he had.

The ones after that came a lot easier.

Chapter 2

Ten minutes later Jeff was in the kitchen, stuffing the remnants of his dwindling food supply into his son's backpack. There wasn't much left, just some half-eaten boxes of cereal and dry noodles to gnaw on. That was what it had come to. It was why he had left the house to search for supplies. Jeff blinked as he suddenly realized his family had died for a few cans of beans and some crackers.

He angrily jammed the last of his meager rations into the bag and ran toward the steps leading to the second floor. From the back of the house came the sound of more glass shattering. He had covered the big picture window with plywood and it was holding for the moment. The wood vibrated under a barrage of hammering fists but stayed in place. He rushed up the stairs, taking them two at a time.

Glad to get away from the stench of infection filtering through the windows and doors, he took a right into his office, trying his best to ignore the shattered door on the left side of the hallway and the carnage that lay beyond it.

Rummaging through one of his bookshelves he found a souvenir mug and dumped its contents on the desk. Sifting through the coins, bits of paper, and other faint memories, Jeff spotted a tiny key. Grabbing it, he went to the top of the bookshelf and pulled down a lock box. Unlocking it quickly he spotted the gun. The tiny pewter weapon with the black grip was still in its original box. Jeff looked at the etched wording on the barrel: *MODEL RAVEN CAL-.25 AUTO.* He picked up the small clip sitting next to it and slid it into the gun. He nearly laughed. It was a pea-shooter that carried a meager six bullets in the clip. Shoving it in his pocket, he promptly forgot about it.

Moving to the other side of the desk he began to rifle through it. After grabbing a pocket knife and the Mag-Lite, Jeff looked around his office. That was it. He sighed and shook his head. He was no survivalist but a baseball bat, a purse gun, and heavy flashlight probably weren't going to get him very far.

As he turned to leave he spied something else on one of the book shelves and stared at it for a moment. It was the photo of Ellen and the kids on their last vacation at the lake. Jeff remembered taking the picture. It had been early, maybe about six a.m. Ellen had been trying to drag the kids out of bed for ten minutes. They didn't want to go out on the boat and didn't want to swim. They just wanted to sleep. She started tickling them and after a couple of minutes the three were wrestling in a tangle of sheets, screaming and giggling. Taking the picture had been spontaneous; Jeff had grabbed the camera out of his bag without thinking. They were smiling, laughing, their eyes lost in a moment of pure bliss. When he showed Ellen the picture she hated it. Her hair was a mess and she had no makeup on. When he put it on display in his office she was angry until he explained. *"Everything that matters to me is in that picture. It's you and the kids, happy. That's all I care about."* She never said another word about it.

Jeff's fingers quivered as he traced the outline of their faces. Another angry scream filtered from below and he tore his eyes away from the picture. Cramming it into his pocket, he headed back downstairs.

It's time to go.

The urgent thought beat out a staccato rhythm inside his head as he made it back to the main floor. Rushing into the garage he could hear the roar outside. They were actually starting to throw their bodies against the side door now. The sound of them crashing against the house was nearly overwhelming but Jeff ignored it and tossed his small amount of supplies into the minivan. Snatching up the baseball bat he ran back inside.

He was out of breath as he got to the front door. Bending at the knees, he tried sucking in as much air as possible and tried to settle down. The noise at the front of the house wasn't nearly as bad. The mob had not spread to the front door yet, which worked well with his hastily cobbled together plan. Bending over, he snatched up the hammer dropped there a few minutes before and started prying at the two by four nailed across the door.

It took some effort but within a couple of minutes the board was down and the only thing that stood between Jeff and the outside world was a deadbolt.

Digging into another pocket he pulled out the key to the car sitting in the driveway. Palming the dark plastic key fob, he pressed the red alarm button. Suddenly, an urgent honking cut through the tumult of screams and howls that had nearly driven Jeff's family mad over the past few weeks. For a moment it seemed as if this new noise, so shocking and ordinary, would overpower all others. But it was not to be. A tide of rage carried the volume of his neighbors above that of the horn as they began attacking the car.

"Stupid mother-fuckers," he snorted with disdain. After listening for a few more seconds he pressed the red button again and the alarm cut off, replaced with the sound of wet slaps on the hood of the Impala. Glass shattered and Jeff could imagine a thick press of bodies trying to get at whoever had been honking the horn.

He strained to hear as much as possible. There was frustration and rage, but more importantly, he heard no one on the porch ready to punch a hole through the front door. Taking a deep breath, he slowly let it out as he scooped up the baseball bat and put his hand on the deadbolt. Turning his head, Jeff took one last look around the house. He wanted to remember it as it had once been and not what it was about to become. Nodding to assure himself, he tried to keep his breathing steady as he turned to face the door.

Flipping the dead bolt, he tensed as his hand slipped down to the knob.

"Well, here goes nothing."

Jeff opened his front door.

Chapter 3

A wall of sound washed over Jeff. The depth of the noise was profound and he felt as if he was on a stage, the world around him vibrating with excitement. His skin contracted around every hair on his body all at once. It was almost painful as the goose bumps puckered his flesh and the sound jarred his bones.

There was the smell as well. It had been out there before, when he had slithered through the neighborhood, but nothing like this. The stench, the miasma from a hundred infected and befouled bodies, had no discretion as it poured over him, baptizing him in its corruption.

Opening the door hadn't drawn any attention but as he let go of the knob it slammed against the wall, making a loud thumping noise as the door slowly began moving back toward Jeff. He jumped slightly and swung his head toward the mass of stiffened bodies milling around his car.

The mob turned as one to stare at him. The sounds, the hissing and moaning, suddenly stopped as the corrupt shifted their gazes from the car they had been demolishing to face the man standing in the open doorway.

None were on the porch. They were busy climbing all over the car, trying to capture the little gremlin inside terrorizing them with its bleating horn. Some were closer, shambling on the front lawn, but were still a few feet away. Jeff's heart raced but it felt like time had begun to slow. His vision dimmed and the dread that had been pouring over him like warm molasses began to evaporate.

Move.

He caught something out of the corner of his eye beyond the crowded front yard. When his eyes tried to follow it, seeking out the blur of motion, it was no longer there. But it *had* been; he was sure. It was something that could move much faster than his neighbors. They were slow and sluggish, but whatever he had seen moved with a fluid grace.

Move!

There it was again, at the back of the crowd but getting closer. He could see glimmers of light flicker between the gaps in the mass of bodies. Whatever was making the shadows dance cut smoothly through the sluggish creatures on Jeff's lawn as it slid closer. He heard a blood curdling scream.

"MOVE!"

He barely recognized his own voice. The fury of the word was jolting; setting him in motion as the mob surged forward, closing the distance to the front door. Stepping back into the house he spent a split second trying to rediscover what had caused the blur of motion at the periphery of his vision, but it was already gone.

The first group of neighbors was almost at the door, close enough that two in front were leaning in to take ragged swipes at Jeff. They missed as he quickly stepped back inside the house. Their groans merged with the others but Jeff could have sworn he heard a different tenor to their gurgling cries. They were excited to be this close to someone still warm and breathing. He continued to move backwards into the foyer.

Turning, he ran to the stairs and jumped onto the couch he had hastily set in front of them, stepping on an arm rest and vaulting over it. He stood watching as more bodies poured in through the front door, scratching and clawing at each other as they tried to force their way through the narrow opening. They were a crazed mob, frothing at the mouth and howling at him. The first few were already at the couch, trying to get over, around, or through it. They smashed, clawed, and tore at it, angry that something stood between them and their prey.

"That's it, you bastards! Come and get me!"

He had to yell to be heard over the pounding fists and squeals of anticipation. The moans were louder inside. But when Jeff spoke they seemed to go still and the noise died down for a moment. He had their complete attention.

He continued to back up the stairs as more bodies crammed into the foyer and spread into the dining and living rooms. He wouldn't be surprised if there were enough of them to fill the entire first floor. One knocked over the vase on the end table near the door and it instantly turned to powered shards underfoot. A few of the ghoulish apparitions appeared to be distracted, wandering toward the dining room table and grabbing at things like they were at a rummage sale. The rest, however, continued to crowd around the base of the staircase, staring balefully up at him. They raised their hands, reaching toward Jeff with unimaginable need.

The weaker ones were crushed underneath the churning mass of bodies as they poured over the couch. It looked like some sort of blender, where whatever was dropped into the spinning vortex was sucked to the bottom to be pulverized, but in this case it was only the smaller forms, children and the mutilated, being sucked beneath the trampling feet.

The first stiff form able to make it past the couch got a shot in the mouth from Jeff's baseball bat. It was a world class upper cut that shattered the woman's jawbone and knocked her back into the crowd. She knocked another person flat and Jeff lost sight of her as she was swallowed in the mass of pulsating bodies. The others ignored her demise as they pressed against the couch. As three more bodies flopped over it Jeff rushed to the second floor landing.

Ignoring his shaking hands and ragged breathing, he pushed the massive bookshelf that stood next to the stairs toward the top step. He had dragged it there a few weeks back as a precautionary measure in case the infected managed to break in the house. In hindsight, it had been foolish to hope that mere furniture could hold back the horde, but he was still glad he had moved it into position.

Jeff felt a white hot flash of fear at the sound of a loud grunt nearby. The infected were almost to the top of the steps. He responded with his own desperate grunt as the bookshelf teetered over and started falling sideways down the steps.

The loud crash he had expected was muffled by the wall of flesh the heavy cherry bookshelf landed on. It smashed into the two leaders of the pack, driving them back into the convulsing crowd. As he watched, Jeff eyes widened in surprise. The six foot tall piece of furniture did not fall to the ground but hovered as the monsters behind it struggled to free themselves of its bulk.

The bodies were piling up behind the bookshelf and he could see it slowly turning like a heavy door being pushed toward the wall. It had smashed a few of them pretty good but was no deterrent to the rest. They were still coming.

As Jeff turned and began running toward the master bedroom he heard a thud as the bookshelf finally hit the floor. They had pushed it out of the way and were on the move again.

He screamed a few expletives as encouragement, though none were needed, before slamming the hollow door to his bedroom shut and clicking the button-lock on the knob. As Jeff moved toward his closet he could hear his neighbors screaming in frustration from down the hall.

Moving past the heavy chair he had put in the closet, he pushed on it, forcing the door shut with its bulk. The large walk in closet went pitch black and he nearly yelped when the first fist slam into the bedroom door.

The darkness felt overwhelming but Jeff knew how

little time he had. He felt his way past a minefield of shoes and piles of clothing strewn on the floor.

Finding the back wall, Jeff dropped quickly to his knees, setting the baseball bat down as he began sliding his hands over the carpeted floor. *Where is it?*

He jumped again as the master bedroom door splintered and quickly broke. The mob was already forcing their way past the shattered remains of the feeble barrier and clambering into the bedroom. They would be at the closet door in less than a minute but that was all the time Jeff thought he needed, if he could ever find what he was looking for.

Cursing under his breath, he began tossing shoes out of the way. He knew the spot on the floor was not covered up but could feel panic setting in as he continued his furious search.

Boom!

Jeff let out an involuntary yelp of surprise as the closet door vibrated in its frame. There were excited moans beyond the door, as if his neighbors knew he was caught like a rat in a trap. It would be mere seconds before he was in their grasp.

"How in the world did you know I was in here, you stupid bastards!?" Jeff screamed as he frantically continued his search. His words echoed in the small, confined space and filtered out into the bedroom, where squeals of delight at hearing his voice cascaded back in on him.

He heard the chair move slightly across the carpet, inching backwards as the press of bodies crammed against the door began forcing their way in.

"I mean, Jesus! You fuckers can't even turn a goddamn doorknob anymore but you can sniff me out in a matter of seconds? What the hell?" Jeff's voice cracked as he spoke, his frayed nerves nearly past the point of no return as he clawed blindly at the carpet.

The chair slid another few inches inward and with it came a splinter of light from the bedroom. Immediately, Jeff saw what he had been searching for, a few inches to his right.

He whimpered in relief as he pulled the hinged door in the floor open.

The clothes shoot was something he had built shortly after they had moved in, when Ellen realized the laundry room was directly below their closet. It made the transfer of dirty clothes a breeze.

He stared down at the washer and dryer. Breathing a quick sigh of relief when he saw that no one had wandered into the small room off the garage, he quickly swung his legs over and down through the hole.

Twisting around as he lowered himself through the narrow opening, Jeff saw the chair get pushed completely out of the way of the closet door. The first shadowy figure stumbled into the room, falling inward, pushed by another four stiffs behind it. Jeff snatched up his baseball bat as he contorted his hips in an effort to get his mid-section through the tight gap in the floor.

His neighbors turned as one toward him, their eyes going wide with excitement as they saw the man trapped in the corner. Their potent smell blasted him, curdling his stomach. It was like a landfill, stockyard, and a mass grave all wrapped up in one. As they reached for him, Jeff screamed and felt something give. The sides of the laundry chute scraped his sides but as he landed on top of the washing machine he heard the spring loaded door on the shoot slam shut above his head.

He slid off the washer. There were cries of outrage from above. They were already scraping at the small door, desperate to open it.

The sounds on the first floor were overwhelming as he stared at the kitchen door. Beyond were those inhuman things...probably more than a hundred. Jeff hoped silently that they were still climbing the steps and cramming themselves into the various bedrooms on the top floor in a futile effort to find him.

He grabbed the gas can he had left in the room and opened it. The smell of the fuel was pure and intoxicating compared to the noxiously rich smell of death now permeating the house. He splashed the flammable liquid on the walls, watching as it ate at the traces of blood the first set of intruders had left behind. He drained the can, splashing the last bit of it on the ceiling, specifically the hinged door above the washer.

The shoot door opened slightly and then slapped back shut. A dark smile crossed Jeff's lips. He had put a set of really tight springs on the sucker to discourage his kids from playing with it. The clumsy bastards upstairs were having a hell of a time trying to get a grip on it because of that.

Setting the gas can down, he picked up the road flare he had also tossed in the room. Cracking the door leading to the garage, he relaxed slightly as he saw that the side door had not been breached. In fact, it appeared as if no one was pounding on it anymore. Wedging his foot in the door to keep it open, he turned to face the kitchen.

There was only one thing left to do.

Pulling the cap off the road flare, it burst to life and startled Jeff with its ferocity. Quickly, he touched it to a rag he had soaked in gasoline that sat on top of the washer and watched it burst into flames. Reaching for the knob on the kitchen door, he opened it just wide enough to slip the flare through. He heard it drop on the floor and quickly shut the door.

Snatching up his baseball bat, he used it to slide the flaming rag off the washer and directly into a puddle of gas on the floor.

"The house is all yours, guys. Enjoy it," he said as he scrambled into the garage. He made sure the metal door was shut tight, knowing it would hold back the flames for a while. As he slid into the minivan he thought about the rest of the gasoline he had drenched the house with, including the kitchen. Along with the propane tanks he had opened in the bedrooms upstairs, it should create one hell of a bang.

Chapter 4

The thin metal garage door gave way faster than Jeff had thought it would. Smashing through, he shot down his driveway and plowed directly into one of his neighbors who had been making their way toward his front door. There was a thud as he connected and then a thump as he ran over the body.

Leaning back, he could see three others closing in on the minivan. Without hesitation he pressed his foot to the gas and twisted the steering wheel slightly. The first debilitated figure was hit square and dragged beneath the rear wheels as he moved onto the street, where he grazed another, sending it tumbling back in the direction from which it had come. Jeff straightened the wheel and flipped the van into drive, giving it gas as he sideswiped the third. Accelerating past the three bodies he stopped suddenly, the anti-lock brakes preventing him from skidding to a halt. He looked back and saw that the two stiffs that had bounced off the van were already getting back up while the third was having a rougher time of it. Its left side was completely crushed but it was still trying to rise, unfazed by the massive trauma the two ton vehicle had caused its body.

Jeff stared at the maimed creature. The power of the hit had ruptured most of its internal organs and there were bits of gut spread several feet behind it. He watched in amazement as it continued to struggle, deliberately trying to raise itself with its one useful arm, but much of its body had been crushed and sealed to the pavement. Staring out the side mirror, he was spellbound by the image as he kept waiting for the movement to stop, but it never got slower. The twisted and damaged form seemed incapable of comprehending that it would be unable to remove itself from the ground without assistance.

The other two were almost to their feet. Jeff gripped the steering wheel tighter and flipped the car into reverse again. This time he floored it. The wheels did not spin but the engine roared and he slammed into the bent over forms before they could rise completely. He kept moving backwards and pointed the van to the spot where his first victim lay.

The vehicle jumped slightly, telling him he had run over the man once again. He hit the brakes and put the van back into gear. This time he moved forward slightly, doing his best to make sure the tire was directly on top of the mangled body.

"Stay down you freak." The words sounded nervous to Jeff. He stopped the van and put it in park. A quick check confirmed that the other two would not get up again and the third was indeed directly beneath him. He heard no more movement.

Shivering uncontrollably, he stared at the dashboard and tried to settle down. He did not want to look up and see how many more ghouls were coming.

Still staring at the speedometer, he felt a thunderous *whump!* Jeff raised his arm instinctively as he saw a bright flash coming from his house. One of the upper-story windows had blown outward and shards of glass were raining down on the minivan, the yard, and the entire street. The van rocked slightly and Jeff ducked as he heard the repetitive tinkling of wood and glass bouncing off the roof of the Odyssey.

He started to lift his head when there was another series of explosions. Bending back over, he let the vibrations roll over him and could have sworn the van slid sideways slightly.

The explosions were muffled and Jeff guessed it was the propane tanks going up. Two were in bedrooms on the back side of the house. He wondered how the backyard looked.

Slowly raising his head, Jeff stared at his house. As he did, another explosion ripped through it, blowing the front door off its hinges as a giant belch of flame spit from the entrance. Fire was everywhere. Smoke was pouring out of the garage as another explosion tore a hole out the side of the house where the laundry room had been. Part of the exterior wall smashed into the side of Mark's house and snapped his split rail fence into kindling. Jeff watched as the flames billowed toward the sky, his pupils growing large with the vision.

He was beginning to feel the heat out on the street, or imagined he did. The sun beat down as he watched, dumbfounded, as fire devoured his home. It was melting everything: the wriggling bodies packed together like sardines inside, the corpses of his family, and all his possessions. It was all gone.

Jeff watched as the flames continued to conquer the structure. Out of the corner of his eye he could see shadowy shapes getting closer. The fire would probably lure them from all over the neighborhood and beyond.

"Let 'em come. Let them see what I've done," Jeff said as he stared at the remains of his house. The bitterness in his voice was thick but the look in his eyes was sad. Digging into his pocket, he plucked out the picture of his family he had taken from his office.

He stared at it, trying to find a measure of peace from the revenge he had gained but couldn't. Raising his finger, he traced the image of Ellen's face; the crazy smile, her hair tousled from the wrestling match with the kids. He studied her, the nose with a slight bend at the tip and the tiny, razor-thin scar on her chin. Suddenly Jeff's hand began to twitch and he pulled his fingers away from the picture and balled them into a fist. He raised it to his mouth and bit into his knuckles.

"I'm so sorry."

He stared at his children, but could not bring himself to touch their faces like Ellen's. His eyes wandered back to her. Jeff bit deeper into his flesh as random thoughts about his wife filtered in and out of his mind. Then the words came again, stifled by the fist jammed in his mouth.

"I don't know what else to do. I don't know where to go. But I-" He closed his eyes tightly and tasted coppery blood as his teeth pierced the skin around his fingers. He unclenched his jaw and freed his hand. Wiping the blood on his shirt he tried to think of what he should say. It seemed ridiculous. His entire family was dead. They were in a place where they could no longer hear him or even cared what he might say. But he was compelled to speak.

"I can't take you with me." He opened his eyes and looked at the picture again. He tried to memorize their features, tried to absorb everything about them that he could in that instant. "I can't be thinking about you all the time. It'll kill me quicker than those things. I just...I just can't."

Jeff's heart raced as he crumpled the picture, the blood from his bite rolling into his hand and trickling onto the photo. He began tugging at his wedding ring. His fingers were swollen so it took some effort but he finally got the ring off. He studied the simple gold band for a moment.

Pressing a button, Jeff lowered the window and unceremoniously tossed the ring and the crumpled picture out on the street. Without looking out as it fell, he rolled the window back up. It was done. There was no relief, only a sense of emptiness in a place that had once been filled.

He was alone.

Chapter 5

"Holy shit!" Jeff yelled as the teenage girl slammed into the hood of the van. He had been far too busy studying the burnt corpses at the entrance of his house and the other bodies coming toward him out of the rear view mirror to notice her immediately. The hope that she might be normal passed quickly.

He glared at her and wondered why he had assumed she was a teenager. The outfit fit the profile but it was still hard to tell. Her skin was mottled with grey and green battling it out to see which could grab more attention. He could tell that the hair she had was once long, straight, and blond. Now those golden tresses were caked in blood and just like a chemo patient were falling (or had been pulled) out in several large clumps. Her left breast was exposed, the nipple bitten off, her belly shirt in tatters. Multiple piercings ran down both ears and Jeff thought he caught a glimpse of a shiny stud in her tongue. There was a glint of silver in the blackened stump wriggling around in her mouth.

Her goo-encrusted eyes never left Jeff's as she attempted to climb on the hood of the van. It was hard to tell if they had once been blue or green with the milky cataracts covering them. The pupils remained their original black and stood out against the pale background.

It was too late to plow her down since she was already on the bumper, reaching for the windshield. Her desiccated fingers scratched at the metal, trying to get at him. Jeff rubbed his eyes wearily as the girl began to gain traction and started climbing up the hood.

There was a moist thud as her fist hit the window with little power behind it. The moan that escaped her lips made Jeff giggle uncontrollably. "This shit is just too goddamned funny!" he shouted as she started going at the window with both hands. The pus and blood from her mouth and torn breast was leaking all over the front of the Odyssey. As he watched the spectacle he began to feel like he was losing his mind.

The other creature that showed up at the passenger door was less of a surprise. The crowd was still sparse but starting to bunch up around the house.

He looked in his rearview mirror, ignoring the two ghouls on top of him for a moment, and did a double take. Swinging around to stare, his jaw dropped.

They were coming out of the house.

Jeff ignored the pounding on the glass and watched as a handful of his neighbors separated from the conflagration and began moving slowly in his direction. He scanned the gaping maw that had been the front of his house and saw that there were others behind them, crawling and scratching as they pulled their charred remains out of the fire.

Much of their skin was burnt away and even the ivory white bones underneath appeared singed and blackened. They were blind, their eyes gone, boiled inside their skulls until they had burst and even the residue had melted. One, still on fire, somehow managed to stumble out to the lawn. It moved randomly, its internal radar out of whack as it staggered this way and that. It left a trail of liquefied organs everywhere its feet touched the ground.

Jeff giggled again at the absurdity of it all. His laughter was drowned out by the rain of blows hammering down on the van. Another slack, mindless neighbor had joined the other two in their pursuit of fresh meat and was actually shaking the vehicle.

He glanced over to the passenger side where two of the rotting monsters were trying to get at him. One was a man with an eye dangling on a stalk of nerve tissue halfway down his face. A good chunk of flesh was ripped clean off his skull. The bone was not bleach white but had a reddish-yellow hue to it. The flesh on his fingers had swollen and popped and the bones sticking out were leaving scratch marks on the window.

The one pushing on the minivan was a real anatomy lesson. Some organs were missing along with most of its rib cage but the rest were on display. His face was covered in ragged strips of flesh as if giant claws had sliced into it. There was a great deal of dangling meat from his chest cavity and gravity was pulling it toward the ground as he continued rocking the van back and forth.

Shaking his head, Jeff hit the gas pedal and the Odyssey shot forward, shedding the freaks trying to smash their way inside. The girl up front had latched onto the hood so he spun the wheel with the hope of watching her slip off the side. When she refused to relinquish her hold he shook his head in frustration.

"Come on, honey! I ain't *that* good looking!"

Speeding away from the others, he rolled down the street toward the entrance of the subdivision. When he reached an area clear of pedestrians he skidded to a halt. Even with the violent motion of the van the girl remained affixed to the edge of the hood.

Filled with inexplicable rage, Jeff screamed at her. "So you want play, little girl? Huh? Well, I'm ready to play!" As he spoke, he snatched up his baseball bat, opened his door, and jumped out of the van.

Pointing the bat at the teen, who was finally relinquishing her hold on the hood, Jeff moved around the door. "Your ass is mine, bitch!"

Before she could slide off the first swing struck her arm and there was a distinctive crack as the bone broke. Not surprisingly, the girl seemed unfazed as she plopped to the ground and tried to lunge at Jeff.

Taking a back handed swing at her face, his bat struck her in the forehead, knocking her off her feet. Immediately, the girl began crawling to her knees.

"Stay down, you fucking monster!" Jeff punctuated the words with a solid kick to her ribs. The force of the blow moved her sideways a few inches but didn't deter her. As she growled he kicked her in the stomach this time and heard the hiss of air shooting through her clenched teeth. He watched as she used her arm he had broken to try levering herself to a standing position.

Leaning against the van, Jeff shook his head in disbelief. Her arm was bent at an odd angle and it appeared as if part of the bone was threatening to tear through her mottled flesh, but the teen was almost standing. Snarling, she planted her feet and prepared to charge.

Gripping the bat in both hands, Jeff swung away. She was moving when he did it and the combination of the power of his swing and her forward motion nearly tore her head from her neck as the bat connected with her right temple. Whatever intelligence remained in her eyes blinked out as the flesh at her throat tore free from her neck and her skull shattered at the point of impact. By the time her body hit the street she looked no different than any of the other rotting corpses littering the neighborhood.

Staring down at his latest victim, Jeff tried to catch his breath. He was not quite sure how to feel as he watched a puddle of fluid that could not rightly be called blood pool beneath the teenager's rent neck. Her dead eyes stared up at him mockingly.

Gripping the bat even tighter, he raised it up with the intention of slamming down on her again and again, until those hateful eyes were obliterated. But before he could take another swing the howling and moaning around him increased dramatically.

He was surrounded. They were still spread out but closing in on his position, coming from all directions. Jeff swallowed hard as he realized how stupid it was to have gotten out of the van.

Suddenly, a small shadow flashed across his eyes and he turned. He wasn't sure what it was but as he looked between two houses, blinking as he tried to adjust his eyes in the bright sunlight, he couldn't see anything. Still, it reminded him of the blur of motion he had seen from his front porch not so long before. For an instant Jeff thought that perhaps it was just some big dog or other animal running wild but dismissed the idea almost immediately. The infected were indiscriminant about what they devoured. He had watched a pack of them tear apart Daisy, a neighbor's Bassett Hound, less than a week before, from his bedroom window. When they were done even the dog's bones were gone.

Slipping quickly inside the minivan Jeff knew only two things for certain: it was time to leave the subdivision and he had no desire to find out what was out there moving so fast he could barely catch a glimpse of it.

As he got rolling again there were plenty of abandoned cars clogging the street along with the predators following in his wake. He drove carefully to avoid both.

"Sorry folks, but I'm not on the menu tonight." Jeff smiled and waved, staring out the window at the milling people on the street along with the ones climbing out of broken windows and through shattered doors of the houses along his route. There seemed to be an endless supply of them.

"It's like I'm the freakin' Pied Piper," he laughed as he stared out the rearview mirror at his trail of followers.

As Jeff's eyes moved back to the road he slammed the brakes, coming to a sudden halt. He groaned as he looked ahead. A multi-car pileup had clogged up the entrance to the subdivision. As the van idled, he stared at the series of sedans and trucks jammed next to one other. They were not only on the street but on the grass as well. One car had plowed into the *"Welcome to Stonehill"* sign out by the main road and half its bricks had fallen on the hood of the vehicle.

Scanning the mess, Jeff's eyes narrowed as he realized it wasn't just some simple twenty car pileup he was looking at. Cars in accidents didn't line up perfectly with one another. Someone had parked them there to barricade the entrance.

"Great...just fucking great," was all he could say as he scratched his scalp in consternation. It didn't take much to guess that the other entrance, on the far side of the vast, sprawling neighborhood, was probably in similar shape.

Leaning back, Jeff felt like bellowing in rage. He had a full tank of gas and nowhere to go. Somebody had decided to quarantine his neighborhood while he had been hiding inside his house over the past several weeks. As he sat and fumed he wondered if it had been done by someone trying to keep the infected out...or in.

Listening as the crowd got closer he reflected on his situation. His family was dead and his house was a pile of ashes. He had barely made a dent in the rabid population with his little fireworks display and all he had to defend himself was a baseball bat and a pistol about as impressive as a water gun. To top it all off there was a huge entourage of rotting bodies following him, ready to tear him limb from limb the moment he stepped back outside the van.

As he sat and fumed, Jeff's eyes narrowed as a he latched on to an idea. Slowly, he leaned forward in the driver's seat and looked outside. His eyes darted from the rearview to the side view mirror. As he watched the arduously slow crowd continue to get closer he shook his head and laughed.

"Holy shit, I *am* the Pied Piper!" he exclaimed, grabbing the steering wheel and hitting the gas. Turning, he headed back inside the subdivision.

After more than a minute of slow driving and watching more and more of the stench ridden maniacs fall in behind, a smile grew on Jeff's face and there was a gleam in his eyes.

"You've totally lost your mind, Mr. Blaine."

The words were filled with self-doubt but also an undertone of awe. He couldn't believe what he was doing but felt a rush from the freedom his actions were giving him. He had been a prisoner for so long it felt great to do something so completely irrational. He took a deep breath and the air felt clean and crisp in his lungs.

A few minutes later, after several u-turns, Jeff had rounded up a crowd rivaling the one that had entered his house. He gunned the engine and watched as the loose group of bodies grew smaller in the rearview mirror.

Moments later he couldn't see them anymore as he hit the end of one of the streets in his neighborhood. He was at the bottom of a hill and the crowd following was at the top. He could not see them yet but knew they were still coming. The idle of the engine kept the sound of their screams and moans at bay for the moment

Jeff turned off the ignition. Pushing his door open, he grabbed the keys out of force of habit. Stepping onto the asphalt he looked up the hill. Ducking back into the van, he grabbed his baseball bat.

The houses surrounding the intersection were no different than the ones on his street, with plenty of shattered windows and smashed in doors. There were no infected nearby but plenty of their handiwork. A few corpses, half-eaten, littered both the yards and the street. Ignoring the remains, Jeff climbed to the top of the van.

He was almost hypnotized by the distant noises of the crowd. When they were this far off it wasn't such a fearful thing, just the distant rumble of thunder lazily threatening to roll in.

As he waited for the crowd to appear he barely noticed the sound of a garage door opening behind him. At the same instant, the first of the infected crested the hill.

Chapter 6

Jeff tensed and swung around when he heard the faint noise, fearing he had missed one of the ghouls in his cursory search.

"Hello?"

A woman stood underneath a raised garage door staring at him. Jeff blinked rapidly, trying to comprehend that she had just spoken. The infected didn't speak.

He reached up to shield his eyes from the sun, thinking perhaps that she was a mirage. When she began to wave feebly at him he blinked several more times as he tried to come to grips with the fact that she seemed very real.

"Hello?" she repeated. The voice was timid but louder now. It was raspy, as if it had not been used in a long time.

Jeff jumped down from the van and began moving toward the woman. The shock of hearing someone else speak had already passed. The words were barely audible but the voice stood out like a pure note of music in a world filled with static. She looked tiny from a distance but he suspected his perception wouldn't change as he got up close. She was emaciated, the bones in her face and arms prominent.

As he got closer she took a few tentative steps back until he slowed, shaking his head and raising his hand in what he hoped looked like a peaceful gesture. It must have worked because she stopped moving, a curious and timid look on her face.

Picking up speed again, he hoped she understood the need for urgency as he took a quick glance at the hill. When he looked back toward her he saw that she had not sunk deeper into the garage, which gave him a boost of confidence. As he came within a few feet he gave her a closer look.

Perhaps she had been attractive once but now looked barely better than the creatures crawling down the hill behind them. Her hair had probably been cut in a bob but it was hard to tell since the light brown locks were matted and stuck out in various directions from her head, like antenna. Her skin was tight on her bones and her olive coloring had turned the tint of spoiled milk. Her lips were cracked and dried and her arms and hands had no meat on them. Her clothes hung off her small frame and Jeff knew he would be able to count each one of her ribs with ease if they were visible.

"They're coming."

Her voice suddenly sounded a lot firmer. She was looking past him, up the hill, just as he had a moment before. The haunted look in her eyes sent a chill down his spine.

He nodded. "I know," Jeff acknowledged as he too glanced at the encroaching doom. "We have to get out of here."

He tried to break into a smile but faltered. "I can't believe someone else is alive."

He did his best to make his voice calm and soothing. The woman's gaze snapped away from the crowd and she looked him in the eyes. She appeared to be confused, terrified, and unsure of what to make of Jeff.

He extended his hand slowly. She looked down at it, examining the dirt that ran in lines along his palm. "My name's Jeff." Her eyes darted to his face and then back down to his hand again.

"We have to go. *Now.*"

As she continued to stare he added a "please" in a pleading tone and thrust his hand at her emphatically. She looked as if she would prefer to bolt like a deer into the woods rather than touch it. Shaking her head slowly, she began inching into her garage again.

Impulsively Jeff dropped the bat and grabbed her by the shoulders. A small yelp passed her lips and her eyes bulged in terror. That was all she could muster. She made a weak effort to break free as he shook her.

"Hey! HEY!"

Her head was turning toward the garage and Jeff felt the hairs stand up on his arms as he heard her moan. It sounded far too similar to the infected for his taste. He almost let go, fighting revulsion as she fought to break free. Instead, he strengthened his grip. A moment later, when his hand came up quickly and slapped her hard across the cheek it surprised him almost as much as it did her.

Suddenly, the woman stopped struggling and moved her hand to where he had hit her. Her eyes glinted will full blown terror as she stared at Jeff.

"Listen," he said. His voice was surprisingly calm. "We have about a minute until those things get here. I don't plan on sticking around and neither should you."

Jeff began pulling her out of the garage. Still stunned, she followed for a couple of feet as if her legs were disconnected from the rest of her, moving of their own volition. He turned her to face the street. She nearly stumbled but kept her feet under her as he stabbed a finger up the hill.

"See! Here they come!" he practically screamed in her ears. The sharp words appeared to be having a stronger effect than the slap did.

The infected had closed much of the distance, making steady progress down the hill. A few had fallen and disappeared beneath the steady churn of feet. There was no concern for the lost ones as the others continued trudging toward the van. They tripped and staggered over torn limbs and dragging entrails. Even at a distance the two survivors could see the mold and rot gripping the festering forms. Tattered pieces of clothing stuck like a patchwork to their bodies, saturated and caked with dirt and fluids not easily identified. On the whole they were sexless. A few strands of hair floated like a halo on a woman's head and a few tattered breasts were on display, but most were too mutilated to make any distinctions. Many had distended bellies filled with bits and pieces of those they had mauled and devoured. It was a twisted parody of pregnancy and it went even further in making them all look similar. The variety of grays and greens coloring their skin blended together to insure there was no distinctions amongst them.

Jeff wrenched the woman around to face him and forced her to look into his eyes. "*Please.* Come with me." The words, spoken precisely and with special effort to hide the unhinged terror he was starting to feel, hung in the air between them. He could see the turmoil on her face as she debated whether or not to trust him. Gritting his teeth, he almost missed the slight nod when it finally came.

Jeff could feel relief flowing through his body at her response. He spared her a brief smile as he leaned down to pick up his bat. Retaining a grip on her hand he turned back toward the van, dragging her behind him. He continued to fear the approaching hoard but was surprised to discover he was more concerned about having someone to watch over again. Someone who did not trust him and would probably run the first chance she got. The quicker she was in the van, the better.

The weakened woman fought to retain her balance as they crossed her neighbor's lawn at the corner of the street. As she glanced around, she could see more infected coming toward them from other directions besides the huge mass of bodies stumbling down the hill. She swung her head from side to side, watching for those that might be getting too close and tried to break into a run toward the van as panic set in. Jeff also noticed the newcomers and his grip tightened on the bat and her shoulder simultaneously. There was too much of a chance of her falling to the asphalt in her weakened state to let go. They were running out of time.

As they got close to the van he was forced to finally release her as he pulled the keys out of his pocket. He punched a button on the key fob and thanked the gods of modern technology for automatic sliding doors. It opened slowly and the woman practically flew toward it.

Jeff made for the front door and was reaching for the handle when something heavy smashed into his back.

Chapter 7

Jeff's feet got tangled up as he fell to his knees. Ignoring the jarring pain he used his momentum to slide forward. His heart felt like exploding in fear from the sensation of a wet slap of a hand on his shoulder. Slamming into the front quarter panel, he did his best to twist away from the assault.

The scream from the woman inside the van jarred him worse than his fall. Doing a tuck and roll, Jeff could hear the grunt of his assailant as it tried to latch on to him again.

He somehow managed to elude the man's grasp as he bounced back to his feet and attempted to regain his balance. Backpedaling slightly as his feet finally gained traction, he found he was now in front of the van. The catcalls and howls of the approaching crowd sounded close but he was more focused on the homicidal madman three feet in front of him.

The rotter's arms were ready to wrap him in an embrace while its mouth worked at building up whatever counted as saliva to the infected. It lumbered forward and Jeff feigned a move, committing to the effort but pulling back at the last instant. The creature over extended as it lunged for him and instead grasped empty air. It nearly toppled but stutter stepped and kept its balance. Jeff had somehow managed to retain his grip on the baseball bat during his tumble and swung it back handed at the ghoul. The man crashed heavily to the ground with a muffled thud after the bat connected with the top of his skull. Jeff knew the blow had only grazed it and did not hesitate. He adjusted his stance and brought the bat down again. Festering grey matter burst from its skull.

Looking up, Jeff could see the crowd was only a few seconds away. He had no idea how he had missed the old man sneaking up on him but wiped the puzzled thought from his mind. Rushing around the minivan, he dove into the driver's seat and slammed the door shut. Reaching for the ignition, he stared at it dumbly and felt his entire body go cold with fear. *The keys.*

His mind raced and he immediately realized that they had been in his hand when he was attacked. He had kept a hold of the bat but dropped the keys.

"Fuck!" Jeff screamed in a panic as he turned to leave the van. The sight of three of the infected a few steps away halted his progress. There was no place to go. The van was surrounded.

"You dropped these."

Jeff jumped at the timid voice. He spun his head, having forgotten about his passenger and thinking one of those lunatics had gotten inside the van.

When he realized who had spoken he unclenched his fists. Seeing that she was holding his key chain in the palm of her hand, Jeff felt the urge to plant a big sloppy kiss on her lips. Instead, he grinned wildly and scooped the keys up, fumbling with them until his fingers found the long, slender one with the Honda logo on it.

He nearly let the key fall through his fingers again when the first fist smashed into the hood. Another ear-piercing scream from his passenger did not help either but he managed to hold on and direct it toward the ignition. Jamming the key home, Jeff barely waited for the engine to turn over before slamming the gearshift into drive.

The twosome was pushed back in their seats as the engine roared and the minivan forced a cluster of bodies out of its way. The echo of slapping arms, legs, and other body parts on sheet metal was loud as the vehicle shot forward. Spinning the steering wheel wildly, Jeff began dodging random strays in front of the hood.

Clear of immediate danger, he let the breath out that he had been holding and slowed the van down. They were safe for the moment but he knew as he looked out the rearview mirror that the angry mob would not stop chasing them. True to form, they were marching behind the van, trying to catch it.

As he continued looking in the rearview mirror Jeff saw the face of his passenger pop up, blocking his view.

"Please...can we get out of here?" He turned his head as she spoke, her words tinged with fatigue and desperation. There was a worn out look in her face, a look that told him a great deal about what she must have gone through. But on closer examination there was a gleam in her eyes that took him by surprise. He was not sure what it signified, but he hoped it meant his new partner wasn't ready to give up just yet.

When he did not answer immediately, she pointed down the street.

"This is a dead end."

Jeff turned to follow where her finger was pointing. He could see the end of the street around a curve in the road. The subdivision was large but this was the edge of it. This particular street ended in a Cul de Sac. He already understood that there was nowhere for them to go up ahead and that there was a wall of infected bodies closing in behind them.

He also knew that behind several of the houses in the Cul de Sac was a retaining wall with a twenty foot drop.

"You have to turn around...get past them somehow. This street ends-"

"I know. It ends up ahead. I got it."

"Then turn around before it's too late!"

Jeff was surprised to hear strength in her voice. She had gone from a squeaking mouse to a roaring lion in an instant.

Shaking his head quickly to stave off further protests, he responded. "The exits to the subdivision are blocked off...a bunch of cars and trucks are piled up." He waved his hand in negation. "We're stuck for now."

Jeff could hear her slump in her chair and hoped the conversation was done or at least the potential debate that was starting to brew up. He was not prepared to explain what he had in mind just yet.

The respite lasted only a few moments.

"So what good is heading toward a dead end going to do us?" The question hung on the air and he cursed silently. "I mean, shouldn't we be trying to find a way out of here? There's no way we can drive out of the neighborhood down this way...there's too many trees and there's this wall-"

"Yah, I know about the wall!" Jeff spat out, hating it as the anger rose up in his voice. Calming himself, he kept the pace of the minivan slow and steady. They would be in the Cul de Sac shortly.

"Look, I understand this is a dead end and I know all about the wall. I realize this entire area is infested with those things. But I also know we won't survive that long if all we do is drive around in circles until we run out of gas."

The van came to a stop next to one of the houses in the Cul de Sac. Jeff put the vehicle into park and turned to face his passenger just in time for the assault.

"Are you kidding?"

Jeff's eyes went wide, surprised at the growling tone coming from her throat. He opened his mouth but no words came out.

"I stepped out of my house for this?! After all this time, when I was safe inside? Just so some idiot can get me killed at the end of my street instead of letting me starve to death in my own bed? Jesus Christ!"

"Now wait just a second!" Jeff cut her off, watching as she tore at her short hair, pulling at it with a growing rage. Anger dominated her visage now, her fear in remission.

Hearing the distant wail of the infected behind them, Jeff tried to maintain his composure.

"Have you looked at them? I mean up close?" Jeff spit out the words as he glared at his passenger. The fear returned to her face; the same fearful look she had when he first approached her. A tickle of guilty pleasure ran through Jeff at her reaction.

"Have you studied them at all? Watched them? Figured out what the hell they are or what makes them tick?! Because I sure the hell have!" He tried to control the volume of his voice but it grew louder with each word.

Suddenly, and quicker than Jeff could actually see, her fear was gone again, replaced by an even greater anger than before. Her eyes radiated with it.

"Them?" She tossed her head back. "You mean those monsters that tore apart my neighbors? The ones that *killed* my husband? YES! I *have* looked at them, you bastard! I know what they are! But tell me, please, what the hell does that have to do with us being stranded on a FUCKING DEAD END STREET?!"

It was Jeff's turn to be speechless as he tried to absorb the verbal assault just laid on him. He could see tears rimming the eyes of the young woman he guessed couldn't be much older than twenty five. She rubbed at them angrily; embarrassed he had elicited them from her.

He closed his eyes and his shoulders slumped as he began to feel about two inches tall. Up until that moment it had just been him and a desire for vengeance against the infected. There had been no room for anything else inside his head. Even after saving this poor wretch of a woman and dragging her into his van he had not given much thought to what she must have gone through as the world around them collapsed.

As Jeff sat halfway out of his seat trying to figure out how to apologize the sound of her fumbling with the door handle made his eyes pop back open.

"No! Wait! STOP, please!"

He grabbed for her wrist as he pleaded with her. The awkward embarrassment at how he had acted mixed with cold panic at her attempt to escape. She attempted to dodge him but he was too fast. It was when he got a loose grip on her wrist that she punched him. It grazed his chin, surprising him. Jeff let go, staring at her in shock. Her hand went back to the door and she twisted the handle. It began to slowly open. She pushed on the door but it wouldn't move any faster.

He recovered quickly, spinning her around. Before she could attack again he wrapped her hands in his and shook her, rattling her teeth. "Please! Listen to me. You *can't* just run away. There's nowhere to go. There's nothing left out there!" Pausing, Jeff caught his breath in an effort to calm down. Getting worked up was doing neither of them any good. "They're coming for us, yes. I know that. But if you run now, you *will* die. You'll become one of them..."

He moved one of his hands up to her face slowly and carefully, even as she flinched away. When he gently caressed her cheek and gave her a small, sad smile, she relaxed slightly.

"I can't fight them *and* you. If you run now, they'll follow you. I'll live and you'll die. It's that simple." He stared into her eyes, loosening his grip on her hands. She was still angry and terrified but at least she was listening. "I plan on surviving, with or without you."

Jeff let her hands go. The door was wide open and they could both hear the moans getting closer. "Together we can make it, but you have to trust me." The last words were barely above a whisper.

She glowered at him and did not respond immediately, forcing him to bite his tongue and wait as the cries of hunger grew loud behind them.

"Okay." Seeing the doubt in Jeff's eyes at her response she repeated herself. "OKAY!" It was clear she was still angry with him but it would take a back seat to survival for now. That would have to be good enough.

"So what are we doing?"

She had calmed down significantly. Shivering slightly, there were goose bumps on her arms. It was a thick, humid summer day and Jeff knew she wasn't cold, just afraid. That was something he could handle.

His eyes sparkled as he answered her. "I have an idea."

Chapter 8

The retaining wall at the back of the Cul de Sac had a twenty foot drop-off to a field dense with wild grasses riding in clumps and spreading off into the distance. A small wooded area surrounded the field in a fifty foot semi-circle that swept around until it met the walls on both sides. It was a dried out hunk of hard top with clumps of weeds and an exorbitant amount of mosquitoes. Trees surrounded the area and soil was elevated at the tree line, giving it a scooped out, bowl-like appearance. The wall ran the length of three properties and tapered off at the edges as the soil and trees merged with the top of the wall. There was a barbed wire fence across the top of it with a few "Danger" signs attached.

Jeff spied the drop off in the distance behind the middle house. The backyard was overgrown but essentially pristine. No trees and a nice flat expanse that ended abruptly. He could see trees off in the distance, beyond the property line, but not the sudden drop off that had nothing more than a raised concrete lip indicating its demarcation point. The metal posts driven into the concrete along with the barbed wired attached to them was virtually invisible from in front of the property. The houses to the left and right had fences surrounding the back of their lots-big square barriers stretching all the way to the wall.

Reaching for the glove box, he pulled something out and jammed it into his pocket before stepping out of the van.

Leaning in for his bat, he motioned for his passenger to join him. She hesitated, biting her lip nervously before seeing that Jeff was leaving with or without her. She slipped out and followed him toward the side of the house with no fence.

Moving toward the door leading to the garage, he motioned for her to stay back as he raised the baseball bat and peered through the window.

She stood with her arms crossed and rubbed them continuously as she bounced on her heels, searching the area for movement. Her eyes gravitated back up the street, where she could hear more than see the mob coming for them. There were no immediate signs of danger elsewhere. With the thick trees and drop off surrounding the dead end, it seemed as if they were sheltered on several sides from the approach of more infected. But with the way things were going she was beginning to think being boxed in was a more accurate description of their situation.

The sound of shattering glass made her turn and she saw Jeff had broken one of the window panes on the door. He was already reaching in, twisting the dead bolt. He went inside quickly, taking the bat with him. She followed as he slipped into the darkness of the garage.

"Perfect".

She heard the single word as she stared inside the gloomy room. Jeff was taking an extension ladder off one of the walls.

"Can you give me a hand with this?" She paused as he spoke, her eyes wide with confusion.

"Come on!" Jeff gestured with his head, encouraging her to grab the front end. "Let's get it outside and then let me take the lead."

They moved carefully from the garage, the ladder barely clearing the ground on the side she carried. Grunting with the effort, the sickly woman held on tightly.

"Good. Just keep up with me." He swung his end around and headed toward the backyard.

A puzzled look crossed her face. All she could see was

a backyard surrounded by fences with the drop off beyond that. She tried to slow down and nearly tripped as Jeff kept going. "Could you tell me what the hell we're doing, please?"

He stopped and carefully set the front of the ladder down. She hissed in relief and followed suit. The sweat was pouring off of her in the mid-afternoon heat and her breathing was heavy.

"I am going to take a pair of wire cutters and cut that barbed wire fence. Then we're gonna drop this ladder down the retaining wall."

The slight woman looked at Jeff as if he was speaking in tongues. He made a pretty educated guess as to what was going through her mind and could almost see the gears whirring behind her eyes. He decided to explain before she drew her own conclusions.

"We're not striking out on foot. We're just going to lure them down there," he said, pointing past the retaining wall to the pit beyond. "And once they're down there, we can circle back to the neighborhood...without them following."

Jeff watched her eyes widened. They had a mesmerizing quality to them. He was prepared for her to erupt again, like she had in the van, so he was surprised at how calm she was when she finally spoke.

"And then what?"

He was surprised at the question, expecting more of a protest. He could detect an almost morbid curiosity in her voice and had to resist smiling, knowing it would probably freak her out.

"Then we get the hell out of dodge."

It was clear the simple answer didn't satisfy her from the sudden elevation of her eyebrow. Her hands were on her hips and Jeff was reminded of the look his wife would give him whenever he came up with a half-baked idea.

The background noise was increasing and he tore his eyes away from the woman to look past the houses toward the street. He could see them coming. They were progressing faster than he had expected. A bead of sweat rolled down his forehead.

"Listen!" he shouted as he stepped toward her. She stepped back and he halted. This time it was not skittishness, just skepticism that kept her from allowing him to get any closer.

"I told you that you needed to trust me." He sighed and looked at the ground, unable to endure her judgmental glare any further. He had no idea what he was trying to do or if it would work but couldn't have her see the doubt in his eyes or they would both be lost. He shook his head. "Look, this may be crazy but it's all we've got. If we don't get these...these diseased monsters out of our way we won't make it." He lifted his head slightly and stole a glance at her. His eyes darted back down to the ground as he fumbled for something else to say.

"Fine."

Jeff paused when he heard the word. His mouth slammed shut and he raised his head, the uncertainty on his face apparent. She smiled at him, which was a first. It looked sickly on her face, as if she was nauseated rather than pleased, but that was good enough.

He nodded down at the ladder. "Help me with this?" Rubbing her arms one last time to get rid of the chill, she nodded and picked up her end. Together they maneuvered it toward the wall as she continued to struggle with its weight.

Taking the pair of wire snips he had grabbed from the glove box out of his pocket, Jeff began clipping the wires.

"Could you go grab my bat?" He asked without looking up. He could see her bouncing nervously from foot to foot out of the corner of his eye and hoped the minor chore would keep her occupied until he was finished.

He could see her hesitate before turning and stopping again. He ignored her as best as he could to focus on the fence. She would go or would stay and fidget. Either way he had a job to do.

He did not hear her leave but as he cut through the last

piece of barbed wire he could no longer see her shadow hovering directly behind him.

Jeff grabbed the ladder, dragging it forward. Tipping it over the wall, he carefully let it slide down inch by inch, careful to avoid letting it slip through his fingers.

When he heard the satisfying thump of it landing on the hard surface below, he tested it for stability. Adjusting the top slightly, he put his foot on it, jiggling it. Nodding in satisfaction, he relaxed. They were cutting it close but would make it.

"You ready to climb down?" he asked and patted the ladder, smiling. When he didn't hear a response the smile faded as he turned.

As Jeff scanned the lawn his blood ran cold.

The mob had finally caught up with them and was beginning to stream around the minivan toward the backyard. In front of them stood the other survivor clutching the baseball bat as she slowly backpedaled. The first of the horde were only about fifteen feet from her and closing fast.

"Run!" he yelled at the top of his lungs. His words were swallowed by the screams and squeals, the growls of rage and hunger. He knew she didn't hear him but doubted it would make much difference if she had. She was paralyzed with fear.

Jeff watched as the scene unfolded in front of him. The ladder was directly behind him, offering a quick escape. There was nothing he could do for the woman except get himself killed trying to save her. It was just like it had been at his house with his wife and kids. He would be too late.

All he could do was watch her die.

Jeff felt his pulse race as a low, crazed noise that was not quite a growl escaped his lips. Before he even realized it he was running, his eyes filled with murderous intent.

Chapter 9

There were five closing on her. All Jeff could see were their blood red outlines as raw hatred hammered through him. Passing the woman, he threw his body sideways, blasting into them like bowling pins.

Three fell from the blow. He thought he heard bones snap like kindling but was already rolling out of the way, avoiding jagged finger nails and snapping jaws as he popped up and faced the rotten monsters still coming at him.

"Get down the ladder NOW!" was all he could yell as he dodged the two still standing that were almost on top of him. He had no time to see if his command had been followed as he darted to the left, his foot lashing out at the mid-section of the closest fiend.

It doubled over but the other surged forward and lunged, its eyes wild as it grabbed a hold of his arm. Jeff squealed in surprise at the vice like grip and yanked backwards, avoiding the snapping jaws as the creature bent to take a bite out of his exposed forearm.

His feet tangled underneath him and he began to fall, pulling his attacker with him. Tensing, he waited for the crush of weight to fall on him. When it did, he was surprised how light she was (the long, blood encrusted hair was his only hint as to its sex). He quickly sent an elbow rocketing under her snapping jaw.

"Get the hell off of me!" That was what Jeff heard

inside his head but what came out of his mouth was a garbled mess as he kicked, punched, and scratched at his assailant. She barely weighed anything but her hand was locked on his arm with tenacious determination as she ignored the attacks. Immune to the pain he was trying to inflict, she continued to snap shattered teeth at him.

Grabbing her hair, he pulled her head back and rolled sideways. Moving away from the others and toward the wall, Jeff could feel something hard jamming into his back as he worked to keep the snapping jaws at bay. Sliding off the object that had jabbed him he saw it was his baseball bat.

Driving his head forward, he slammed it into the woman's forehead. There was no time to consider how easily the bone gave way as he felt her grip loosen. Reaching for his bat, Jeff scrambled further back to avoid the tangle of bodies coming for him.

He tried to spring to his feet with the wild hope of making it to the ladder when he felt the teeth biting at his shoulder. Swinging the bat in a wide arc, he turned and was able to get to his feet but missed the arm taking a broad swipe for him.

Jeff's eyes darted back and forth and he lifted the bat, preparing for the next attack. The three misshapen forms he had knocked down were almost back on their feet. The one that had bitten his shoulder was the one he had kicked in the gut. It had over-committed on its attack and had fallen to a knee but was already lunging for him again.

Behind his assailants, just a few feet back, was a second and much larger wave of infected bodies. His eyes wide, Jeff turned and fled as a flood of rotters converged on the spot he had just vacated.

He felt warm relief as he saw a head peeping over the concrete lip of the retaining wall. His scrawny neighbor was still alive.

"Move it, move it!" he yelled as he waved at her furiously with the bat. Her head dipped below the edge and as he got to the ladder he saw her climbing down it rapidly.

Jeff turned and kneeled, feeling his way over the edge to the top of the ladder. Tossing the bat over the side, he began to make his descent. As he did, he stared into the backyard.

They were still pouring in. It looked like every last one of the infected in the world was coming for him. Jeff hesitated, glancing at his shoulder where he had been bitten. A strange sound whistled between his clenched teeth as he saw the rip where his sweatshirt had been torn and soiled by the creature's teeth. The residue from its mouth was slimy black and the smell coming off it was foul. Jeff slid his finger into the tear in the material and felt a surge of relief. There was no blood, no breaks in the skin. The ghoul didn't have the chance to sink its teeth in. It just nibbled on his shirt a bit.

"Come on! Hurry up!" he heard beneath him. He ignored the voice. The crowd still had quite a bit of lawn to cover before they got close to the edge.

The ladder shook as the woman below began to get hysterical.

"Please!" she cried out as Jeff looked down. She was clinging to the bottom of the ladder like a security blanket. He could see it in her eyes: she would lose it if he didn't get down there right away.

"I'm coming, move back a bit," He grumbled and began climbing down. Her expression showed profound relief as she stepped away, wringing her hands.

Jeff hit the ground in a rush. He grabbed his bat and turned, snatching up the woman's hand and they ran toward the center of the flat, dry scrabble field.

Suddenly, Jeff smiled and gave her a quick hug. She was taken off guard by it but when he went to release her she wrapped her arms around him in return, squeezing tight as a single tear rolled down her face.

"What's your name?" he asked. His words were quiet as he barely spoke above a whisper, his lips next to her ear.

Letting go, she pulled back until she could look him in the eyes. With her head cocked to the side, it looked as if she didn't understand the question.

Jeff touched his chest. "My name's Jeff." He smiled, hoping to encourage a response. He had told her his name earlier but doubted she remembered.

Looking up the wall and then back at her savior again, a confused look passed over her face. "Don't you think we should be getting out of here? Can't introductions wait until we're safe?"

Jeff's grin widened as he tried to ignore the tension tattooed on her face. He slowly looked over at the wall and could see the first shadow of movement above. Nodding toward the ladder, he said, "I think we're safe for the moment."

She looked back up in time to see the first of the creatures reach the break in the barbed wire fence. It stopped, looking down at the humans and began moaning, its arms reaching for them. It remained stationary as others joined in. Jeff felt a sudden twinge of doubt in his gut.

Stepping closer, he tried to keep the nervousness out of his words. "Stay back. I might have to get them interested enough to take the plunge."

He could feel a tug on his arm and ignored it. His eyes were glued on his neighbors as they growled and gnashed their teeth.

"Can't we just go?" Jeff barely heard her words as he willed the monsters up above to take one more step forward, just one.

Suddenly the woman was in front of him, grabbing his arm and tugging on it.

"You know, you're one lucky son of a bitch to still be alive. Haven't you figured that out yet?"

Jeff's face showed blank surprise as he stared at her. *Lucky?* How in the hell was he lucky?

"Megan."

"Huh?" Jeff squinted in confusion.

She rolled her eyes. "My name: you asked me my name, remember? It's Megan. Megan LeValley."

Jeff looked down and saw that her hand was out for a handshake. Again, he was flummoxed, unable to say or do anything as he looked at her hand like it was a live wire.

A hiss of exasperation escaped her lips. Dropping her hand, the woman named Megan glared at him. "So, now that we've introduced ourselves can we stop screwing around and get the hell out of here?"

Jeff tried to adjust to the sudden change of temperament in the woman. She seemed to go from extreme to extreme. From docile and timid to angry and now she was trying sarcasm on for size. It seemed to fit just fine.

Jeff broke eye contact with her and looked back at the wall. Before Megan could continue her harangue he pointed with the bat at the ghoulish figures congregating above.

"Look."

Megan's eyes narrowed in anger but she bit her tongue as she indulged his request. She did a double take as she stared at the break in the barb wire. The desire to argue further died as she was transfixed by the image.

More bodies were crowding up against the edge, bumping against those already standing there. From her vantage point Megan couldn't see how many were piling up from behind but the noise was building. The sound was raw anguish and betrayal as the cries reached her ears. She hugged herself, rubbing her arms to try and erase the chill that never seem to disappear. Her eyes darted over to Jeff. He was smiling and seemed relaxed, a look of greed in his eyes as his lips moved silently, speaking to his audience, coaxing them, urging them to *do* something. Shifting her eyes back to the mob, Megan rubbed her arms harder, the chill suddenly much greater.

One finally fell off the edge. Neither Jeff nor Megan could tell if it had decided to walk off, was pushed, or the surging crowd had simply forced it forward. It landed with a sickening thud at the bottom of the pit. Megan covered her eyes as she saw the head connect with the ground. It was so rotten it caved in and the body flopped forward onto its back, its arms and legs spread wide.

"YES! I knew it!" Jeff yelled, pumping his fist and laughing wildly in defiance.

Megan was doing her best to hold back her queasiness as Jeff did a victory dance. Though she wanted to keep her eyes shut, she felt the need to confirm that the person who had taken the leap would not be getting back up. The limbs twitched a couple of times and then stilled. It was dead.

"I knew those uncoordinated dumb fucks couldn't navigate a ladder," Jeff gloated and then pitched his voice toward the crowd. "That's right you stupid fuck-tards! I'm talking about you. Not that you can understand a word I'm saying!"

He laughed maniacally as he egged them on. "Come on down! You're the next contestant on The Price is Right!"

As if in response to his voice, two suddenly fell and five more decided to walk off the edge immediately after. Soon they were like dominoes: more and more taking the plunge, either willingly or because of the surge of bodies pressing up behind them. The moans and various sounds of the fallen mixed and echoed off the wall and through the trees. At first they seemed hesitant but as more crowded around the gap in the wall they came in a steady stream.

Jeff's celebration slowed and then quieted when he saw a child up on the wall. It *had* to be a child-a little girl with a tattered stuffed animal still clenched in one of her small hands. There was a single pigtail still attached to the side of her skull. As she moved, taking her place at the front of the line, her eyes fixed on him. She never looked away even as she landed with a brutal thud on top of the pile of bodies.

They continued to plummet to the ground with a sickening splatter of gristle and guts. A scant few landed on their sides or on top of several other bodies, cushioning the blow. As they tried to get up others flattened them, pushing them back to the ground. The uncut barbed wire and surrounding fences served as a funnel. The infected were forced to jump from the highest point and not a single one tried to use the ladder. Jeff watched as the solid mass up top kept feeding the pit below.

The little girl's jump had dampened his sense of victory and when he saw one of the bodies begin to wriggle free of the mass, he realized the fun was over. One of its arms dangled at an odd angle and it could do no more than crawl but it would gain its freedom soon enough. Jeff took a step back before he even realized it. Others were struggling to squirm free as well and he reached over to grip Megan's shoulder, pulling her away from the pit. He spared a brief glance up to the ledge and saw the crowd thinning out but there were still plenty up there, waiting impatiently to take the plunge.

He turned to face Megan. "Okay." He nodded toward the wall. "This will probably last a few more minutes. I want you to run back to your house through the woods. Be careful though, there might be more of them out there." He saw the fear dawning on her face. "Stay low and keep your eyes open. I'm not staying much longer but if we both leave now the rest won't follow their buddies into the ditch."

Taking a step closer, he shoved the bat into her hands. "Take this. I swear I'll be right behind you." He looked her in the eyes and felt guilt at the fear in them but he wasn't prepared to leave, not just yet. And he knew if Megan didn't leave she would be in hysterics in a matter of moments.

Jeff was prepared to argue with her so he was surprised when all she did was swallow hard, giving the wall one final look before nodding at him. Megan looked like she was going to be sick and he couldn't blame her. This was a gruesome task and there was no need for her to suffer through any more of it.

Suddenly, her arm came up and she slid it around his neck. Jeff was surprised but when her hand touched his flesh he could feel the warmth in her finger tips. Megan pulled him gently toward her. He was even more surprised when she planted a gentle peck on his cheek. "Please be careful. I don't want to lose you too." She let go and stepped back, doing her best to ignore the pit and the bodies falling into it like lemmings.

Jeff gave her a sharp nod and clenched his teeth, doing his best to hide the pain he felt at her gesture of kindness. He turned back to the pit and closed his eyes, still feeling the warmth of Megan's touch. A touch that gave him a sense of hope even as it stung, reminding him far too much of his wife and the tenderness they had once shared.

Feeling helpless, Jeff wanted to scream or cry out, but knew he could do neither. He was lost in a world that was already dead.

Eyes still closed, Jeff continued to listen as the moans diminished and the sound of wet, ruptured bodies smashing into the hard ground echoed all around him.

Chapter 10

Megan cleared the small copse of trees as she kept an eye out for movement. The sounds of the infected faded as she gingerly climbed a fence into a neighbor's backyard. The woods were too thick for her to comfortably navigate and there were far too many places for those *things* to hide.

The house she was behind looked decimated, the sliding glass door shattered with scorch marks on the walls. Megan noticed a few broken chairs inside but tried to avoid looking closer, fearful of what else she might discover. Five minutes later she was huffing and trying to catch her breath as she pawed her way over yet another fence. The baseball bat felt heavy in her hands but she was grateful to have it.

It was hard to tell where she was since the street curved and Megan could not pick out her own backyard off in the distance. It was hard to gauge how much further there was to go. Bending over, she leaned against the fence and sucked in as much air as possible. Her joints ached and muscles burned. She was malnourished, having lived on stale crackers and stagnant water for several weeks.

Stretching her back, Megan heard a satisfying pop. She slowly began pulling herself over the fence, grunting with the effort. She wanted to sit for a little bit but knew if she did she wouldn't want to get back up. Ignoring her agony, she landed heavily in the next yard. Slowly standing, her eyes closed as she tried to stretch her stiff muscles again to avoid getting a Charlie horse. Opening her eyes, she was surprised to find someone creeping out of the back door of the house.

The woman must have seen her from inside and moved to the porch. The split second of excitement Megan felt at seeing another person was replaced with a dull lump of sadness. She was one of them. Her throat had been ripped out, which was why the woman was silent. Her lips were parted and her arms were stretched in front of her as she shambled from the concrete patio to the lawn. Megan thought she saw the white of bone deep in the ragged strips of flesh hanging from the raw wound in her neck. The woman wore a dirty and blood stained housecoat and what had once been fuzzy slippers that were now frayed and black. There were no other visible wounds except to her throat. Her flesh was grey but holding together.

Megan looked at her surroundings as she gripped the aluminum bat possessively. The yard was filled with children's toys and the grass had grown out of control. The far fence looked a mile away. Her eyes darted back to the woman. Megan's mouth twitched as she recognized her.

"Kathy?" Her voice was unsteady.

Kathy Serna was one of the stay at home moms sprinkled liberally across the neighborhood. Childless, Megan had not spent much time with her except for the occasional polite wave as they drove past each other's house or for random chit-chat as Megan went on one of her routine walks around the neighborhood. She felt a glimmer of hope as Kathy's eyes widened at the sound of her voice.

"Kathy? It's me, Megan. Megan LeValley. Don't you recognize me?"

The desperation in her voice excited Kathy. Megan's hope died as the infected woman lurched forward, her dull eyes filled with homicidal glee.

Megan paled at the sight and raised the bat like a samurai sword and began to slither sideways, moving toward the far fence. Kathy was slow but closing the distance far too quickly. She would reach Megan long before she got to her goal.

The desire to run screaming was overwhelming but her body refused to allow her to turn away from Kathy. Megan's legs felt like they were stuck in wet cement.

Kathy was moving slowly as well but still far too fast to give Megan the time she needed to come to grips with the fact that her neighbor wanted to kill her.

Shaking her head in denial, Megan cringed behind the baseball bat. Kathy was almost on top of her.

Suddenly, the bat came crashing down on Kathy's head, knocking her backwards. She stumbled over a tricycle and fell to the ground, her legs tangled up in the wheels.

Megan's jaw looked like it was about to fall off its hinges as she gawked at the bat and then at her hands. Her arms ached from the effort though she barely recalled swinging the bat. As she glanced down at Kathy, who was trying to free herself from her child's trike, she realized the blow had not been very powerful. It was just enough to knock the ghoul down, not enough to cave her skull in. Megan felt a flutter of nausea at the thought but ignored it. The baseball bat was too heavy for her to effectively wield.

She cursed as Kathy untangled her legs and began to rise. Looking at the fence again, Megan thought that she might be able to make it but her brief experience with Jeff had taught her something: these people, whatever they were, never gave up. Kathy would keep coming, even if Megan ran, no matter how many fences there were between them.

Megan's eyes moved to the far corner of the yard, where she spotted a pile of sticks and tree limbs. Moving toward it, she finally turned her back on Kathy. Leaning the baseball bat against the fence, she picked up a thick tree branch that felt light but solid in her hands. Hefting it, she felt a wave of numbness come over her as she turned back to her neighbor.

Kathy had not gone far when Megan came at her with the limb. She put all the strength she could muster behind the blow, connecting across the bridge of the woman's nose.

The ripe pop of cartilage was lost in her grunts as Megan swung again. Her next blow caught Kathy in the ear. She let out little yelps as she continued to batter and beat on the creature.

A minute later, Megan surveyed her handiwork. She wanted to turn away from the mess that had been Kathy Serna's head but discovered she couldn't immediately. It would have been hard to tell where her face had been if not for the position of the body. Megan had kept swinging, relentless, until Kathy had stopped trying to grab for her. Even then, she had kept at it until the tree limb cracked in her hands.

Megan felt faint and teetered for a moment before regaining her balance. Twisting violently away from the corpse, she vomited up the bile scalding her throat. Her gut clenched and she dry heaved for several more seconds, a jagged cry of pain mingling with the retching noises. Stumbling toward the fence, she left Kathy's remains behind.

Whispering an apology to her neighbor as she leaned against the fence, Megan wheezed and tried to gather enough strength to climb over it. The silent apology was not much of a eulogy but it was all she could muster. She wiped at the tears pouring from her eyes furiously, angry at what she had done but even angrier at how she felt about it. *Better you than me, Kathy* ran through her mind like a cold wind.

Megan realized that she didn't feel guilty even with all the anger and sadness swimming around inside her brain. She was still alive and wanted to stay that way...no matter what she had to do. For weeks all she wanted was to curl up and die inside her empty house as the world fell apart outside her window. But the pain in her arms from swinging the tree limb was a not so subtle reminder she was still alive and it was going to take a great deal of agonizing effort to stay that way.

She spared no further glances back at Kathy as she climbed the fence.

Chapter 11

As Jeff navigated the fence line he saw no indications of more infected in the wooded area. Through breaks in the trees he could see more houses in other neighborhoods off in the distance but did not look too closely. He had his own turf to worry about.

The mess he had left at the pit was still fresh in his mind. The crawlers were easily avoided but when one of the ghastly creatures was able to stand up and began moving toward him, Jeff knew it was time to go. As he left, the last of the crowd were still taking the plunge, unfazed by the broken bodies lying below.

He crossed into an unfenced backyard, feeling naked without his baseball bat and nervous about sending Megan on ahead. Too late to worry about that, he spotted the end of the street and her house.

Moving to the front yard he saw no movement...and more importantly, heard no sound. The absence of moans felt strange. Jeff had never gotten used to them, even after all the time he had been forced to listen while stuck in his house. Now that they were gone, he wasn't quite sure how to feel about it.

Staying low, he moved toward the sidewalk. There were still cars in several driveways which he gave a wide birth to, not willing to risk a stray hand lurching out to grab him.

The air was thick with humidity and death. Only a few weeks before Jeff had no idea what death smelled like but now was an expert. It tasted like thick slabs of carrion rolling over his tongue. Everywhere he walked he saw traces and residue left behind by the infected. Puddles of thick greasy liquid and green flesh were deposited in the grass and on the street. More solid matter, blessedly unidentifiable, was occasionally snagged on a low tree branch or splattered across a car window. He did his best to ignore it all as he approached Megan's house.

Her garage door was still open but he did not see her. There was an older green Toyota compact and a red Cherokee parked inside. Jeff paused to scan the shadows and then began walking toward the doorway.

As he moved closer, he spied Megan sitting behind the wheel of the Cherokee, facing away from him. Not wanting to startle her, Jeff stopped before he got to the door.

"Hey."

She turned quickly. Seeing him standing there, she gave a half-hearted wave. Her expression was filled with a deep sadness and Jeff felt a twinge of guilt. It passed and he moved to the car door.

When she did not open it he grasped the handle and pulled on it. Discovering it was locked, he waited for a moment. Megan had already turned back around, as if she had forgotten he was standing there. Tapping gently on the window, he waited expectantly for her to open the door or roll down the window.

When she didn't, Jeff raised his fingers to tap again, worrying that Megan had decided to crawl back into her shell and ignore him entirely this time. Before he could tap the glass the window began to lower.

Turning to look at him with her haunted eyes, Megan spoke first. "I want to leave. Now."

Jeff opened his mouth to respond but she cut him off. "I can't stay here any longer. I don't care where we go but I want to find other survivors."

She looked at him expectantly and after a moment Jeff slowly nodded as he continued to think of a verbal response to her demand.

"Just get in the Jeep so we can get out of here," Megan opened the car door and stepped out, forcing Jeff to back up as she continued. "You can drive...I don't care, but let's go!"

"That sounds like a great idea, Megan, it really does, but I already told you, the roads are blocked, remember?"

A dark look crossed Megan's face as she tried to retrieve the memory of what Jeff had told her about the cars jammed at the entrance of the subdivision.

"I want to leave too, but I think we would be better off waiting until tomorrow. Maybe we can stay in your house tonight?"

Megan's face went pale. Shaking her head rapidly, she took a step back. "No. There's no way we can stay in there. I won't stay here another night." Her eyes seemed to go hazy, as if she was lost in some old memory. An instant later they snapped back into focus and the look she gave Jeff told him it would be pointless to argue.

"Okay, no problem," he said in a placating tone. Jeff paused, thinking. "I'm sure we can find a house around here that hasn't been broken into."

Megan crossed her arms, her expression turning sour.

"We can leave tomorrow. I promise; bright and early," he continued with his appeasing tone. He stepped closer to the petite woman, his hands gently touching her arms. She did not shy away as he continued to speak. "Because if we leave now, it'll be dark before we get very far." He let the meaning behind his words sink in. "I don't think it would be a good idea for us to be out on the road after dark."

Megan absorbed what Jeff said and stood quietly, her expression fatalistic. After a few moments, her features softened.

"What about your house?"

Jeff stiffened, his hands dropping away as his face went blank and emotionless. Megan's eyes widened with curiosity as she waited patiently for a response.

"My house..." he said, shaking his head as he looked off into the distance. He was still trying to wrap his mind around everything he had done. "My house is gone."

Megan waited to see if more of an explanation was forthcoming. When Jeff said no more and his eyes refocused on her, she realized he was still waiting for her response to his suggestion about finding another house to camp out in for the night. Sighing deeply, she nodded.

Jeff smiled and she faintly returned it. He slid past her, between the two vehicles, and leaned into the Cherokee to look inside.

"Is the tank full?"

Megan shook her head. "I think there's half a tank...maybe less."

Jeff gave the SUV a wistful look before he stepped back and carefully shut the door.

"You have anything useful in your house?"

He could see a twitch of anger cross Megan's face and then disappear under a veil of sadness. The question had to be asked, even if it stung. All their possessions, all their cherished memories, were useless anymore. The only things of value that remained were items that might help them survive another day.

Megan walked to the door at the back of the garage, bumping into Jeff as she passed. She looked like she was sleepwalking. Slumping over, she sat on the steps leading into the house and put her chin in her hands. When she spoke her words were monotone, nearly robotic.

"My husband's gun is on a table next to the front door. There's a box of bullets on the top shelf of the closet in the master bedroom. It's behind a stack of shirts. The keys to both cars are on a hook in the kitchen. There are a few cans of food on the counter, but the only water left is in the bathtub."

Jeff's eyes lit up when he heard the word gun. Seeing her downcast expression he worked to keep his own solemn.

"You're not coming in then, I take it?"

Megan did not look up as she shook her head. Nodding slightly, Jeff touched her shoulder as he moved past her up the steps, opening the door into the house.

"Whatever you do, don't go down to the basement."

Jeff turned, looking at Megan from just inside the door. Her back was to him and he could gather nothing from her slumped shoulders. He looked at her for another moment, his eyes showing concern. When she said nothing further, he quietly shut the door and moved into the depths of the abandoned house.

Megan's mind wandered back over her experiences of the past few weeks. Flashes of her husband barricading them inside the house flitted through her mind. She remembered him leaving in the jeep and promising to return with enough supplies to last a month. When he had returned his arm was bleeding from where one of those lunatics had bitten him. She recalled how he begged her not to let him turn into one of those things and slipped her the revolver before passing out from the pain.

The reverie was interrupted by a sound coming from outside the garage. Megan quickly stood, her back pressed against the door. She glanced around, trying to find the baseball bat she had brought back with her. It was sitting in the passenger seat of the Jeep. Her heart raced as she took a single step toward the SUV and then hesitated, fearful that she might alert whatever was out on the street to her presence.

A minute later, with no more sounds coming from outside, she decided to slowly move toward the front of her garage. When she saw the culprit that had startled her, she let out a short embarrassed laugh and moved to the edge of the garage.

An orange housecat was on the porch across the street. It had knocked over a flower pot and was digging into something next to the pile of dirt and broken shards of pottery. It raised its head when it heard her laugh and stared at Megan.

She could feel her stomach churn as she realized what the cat was standing on. As it dipped its head back down and tore into the hunk of meat, ripping a small piece off and chewing it, its eyes never left the woman standing across the street.

Megan could see the blood dripping off its whiskers as it stared at her, indifferent as only a cat can be. Its head dipped back down and it continued digging into its maggoty meal. Its bright coat was tarnished by clots of dirt and a few smears of dried blood, but it looked to be in good health. Plump in fact. The end of the world had been good to this particular feline.

Stepping back into the garage, Megan turned quickly and tried to blot the image out of her mind of what the cat was feasting on.

She nearly jumped out of her skin when she heard the door at the back of the garage open. Jeff walked through the doorway and smiled at her, not noticing her startled expression or her hand gripping her chest as she leaned against the Corolla.

He had a small plastic grocery bag in his hand and her husband's .357 Magnum jammed into the waistband of his jeans. He raised the bag, showing her what he had collected. Megan could see the bullets and the Jeep keys through the transparent material, along with three cans of vegetables that represented the last of her food except for the stale crackers still up on the nightstand next to her bed. They had been her primary sustenance over the past couple of weeks. She could care less if she ever saw another cracker again.

"Can we leave now?"

Jeff was surprised by the irritated question. Megan looked even more agitated than before he had entered the house.

"Uh, yeah." He composed himself and dug into the bag. "We need to get the van first." Seeing Megan's reaction change from irritation to anger, he explained. "The van's tank is full. I don't have an idea where we're going after tonight, but I don't want to do it on less than a full tank of gas."

Megan didn't say anything, her arms once again crossed as she nervously rubbed at them. Jeff was beginning to think it was her favorite thing to do as he jingled the Jeep keys.

"So...you ready?"

The trip took only a couple minutes. With no horde chasing them they were better able to comprehend the extent of the destruction around them. A few houses were in good shape while the majority was ripped apart with windows shattered and doors hanging off their hinges. The two of them cringed as they spotted remains scattered across the front lawns of several homes and silently wondered if they were the owners or just some other unlucky souls caught trying to escape the carnage on foot.

Jeff looked up and down street for movement or signs of life. Seeing none, he relaxed slightly. When he saw the van up ahead he risked breathing a little easier. The vehicle looked to be okay-the mob had not taken their frustrations out on it as they had passed by. Things were looking up.

As he pulled next to it, he glanced into the backyard. His eyebrows furrowed and he shook his head in frustration. Leaning over, he grabbed his baseball bat from off the floorboards. As he did, he felt pressure on his hip. Looking down, Jeff pulled out the revolver he had jammed into his waistband and handed it to Megan. She looked at him, confused.

"Go on over to the van," he said as he left the Jeep and began walking toward the backyard. "I'll be right back," Jeff responded to Megan's unspoken question and then turned to run into the backyard.

There were four still up top. Not a single one was able to stand and they had all been crawling toward the wall before they heard the Jeep pull up. Now they were turning, trying to make the arduous journey back to where Jeff and Megan were. One started in with the grim dirge Jeff knew so well and the other three joined the chorus almost immediately.

Jeff did not break stride as he gripped the bat in both hands and took a golf swing at the closest one. He shook his head as the scarred aluminum made solid contact with its face. The moaning stopped as its neck snapped and its head flopped onto its back. He kicked the next one and several teeth flew out its mouth. Standing over top of it, Jeff let the blows reign down until its head was a puddle of mush.

The two remaining were easily dispatched in the same fashion. Except for the one trying to grab his leg they gave Jeff little trouble. They had all been crippled before he had gotten to them and posed little threat.

Jeff was sliding the bat over the grass, wiping the streaks of gore off of it when he heard more moans coming from over the ledge. Looking back toward the van, he saw Megan standing between the two vehicles, a horrified expression on her face.

Unable to deny his curiosity, Jeff walked toward the wall. Swallowing hard, he peered over the edge. The sound increased as those below caught sight of him.

Broken bodies squirmed and wriggled on their blanket of pulped and decimated corpses. They were tearing each other apart and it was clear from the extent of the damage done that they had been doing so ever since Jeff had left. As bad as they had looked before, they were almost unrecognizable now. Only a few still had the use of their eyes or throats and those that did howled woefully at him. Those with arms raised them, scratching and clawing the others to try and pull their bodies above the pile.

Jeff had to turn away after only a few seconds. He spat on the ground, trying to get the taste out of his mouth as he rubbed his eyes, hoping the image would fade. It didn't and somehow he knew it would stick with him for a long time to come.

Walking quickly back to the van, he ignored Megan as he tugged open the driver's side door and dug in his pocket for the keys. Finding them, he tossed the bat in back and turned the key in the ignition. Megan was in the passenger seat, glaring at him.

"You seem to be enjoying yourself," she spat out. Her expression shifted from frosty irritation to discomfort as she saw the look of pain on his face. Megan's mouth slammed shut and she looked away.

Jeff flipped the van in reverse and backed up. Twisting the steering wheel, he switched gears and they were moving down the road, heading back toward Megan's house.

As they crept down the road, Megan looked over at Jeff again. The pain was gone from his expression but she could still see the ghost of it in his eyes.

"You can't kill them all."

Jeff barely heard the quiet words. He looked at Megan in confusion but she had already turned away, putting her forehead against the window and looking at her house as they passed it by.

Jeff wanted to say something in response, to argue that he wasn't trying to kill *all* of them, but knew it would sound silly after what he had just done.

So instead, he set his sights on the road as they moved up the hill toward the heart of the subdivision. The day was wearing down and it would soon be dusk. They had to find a suitable house to break into to spend the night. The coast still looked clear but Jeff knew there were more ghouls lurking out there, waiting for darkness to fall, so they could begin the hunt.

Chapter 12

"There." Jeff tapped on the brakes. He pointed at a house as they slowed to a stop in front of it.

Like most houses in the neighborhood, it was a two story traditional that had a covered porch running the length of the front except for the connected two car garage. The windows were still intact and Jeff could see the wood nailed up behind them on the first floor. The blinds were drawn on all the second floor windows and there was no obvious visible damage.

He turned off the engine and stared at the house for a few moments.

"So, what do you think?"

Megan shrugged. They had driven down several streets looking for a house and this was the first that looked like someone might still be living in it. Jeff mumbled something about trying to find other folks who had been hiding out like they had and she had nodded politely, though she was skeptical they would discover anyone left in the neighborhood that didn't want to tear their throats out.

Jeff turned and reached back to grab his Mag-lite. Picking up the baseball bat, he opened the door and stepped outside. Surveying the immediate area, he seemed satisfied that they were still in the clear.

Megan got out as well and they met at the front of the van. Jeff looked at her and smiled, nodding at what she was holding. "You know how to use that thing?"

Megan lifted the .357, which looked huge in her hands, and popped the cylinder out and spun it, confirming it was loaded. With a flick of her wrist, it snapped shut and she pointed it skyward.

"My husband took me out to a shooting range a couple of times. I know what I'm doing." The look in her eyes was defiant and Jeff bowed his head and nodded.

"Well, I'll just stick with old faithful then," he said in response, lifting the ball bat. He could feel his small handgun digging into his thigh but ignored it. He wasn't about to pull it out. It would just make Megan laugh.

She began walking toward the house, the gun still pointed in the air as she held it with both hands.

"Uh," Jeff uttered as he ran to catch up with her. "You don't have to do this. I can check the place out myself." Megan didn't spare him a backwards glance as she kept moving forward. He was forced to follow to keep up. "I meant it," he called after her. She was already crossing the lawn headed for the front door. Jeff awkwardly shifted the heavy flashlight to the same hand carrying the bat as he grabbed her elbow from behind and gently stopped her.

Megan turned slowly before she spoke. "Look, I know I was upset with you in the van. I'm sorry about that, but this-" she waved her arms as she looked around, the frustration showing on her face. "It's just hard to comprehend, you know?"

Jeff nodded slowly, a skeptical look on his face.

"I'm still just getting my bearings, okay? But I'm fine, honestly. I can handle this." Megan could see that she had not convinced him entirely. "I am not going to let you take all the risks while I just sit in the minivan."

With her hands on her hips and her elbows jutting out, Megan stared at Jeff until he sighed and nodded again. She could see the slight touch of regret in his eyes and did her best to ignore it.

He looked at the house, sizing it up. "Let's stay

together, but stay a few feet back from me. We need to check things out around back before we try to figure out how to get inside."

Megan nodded and waved him forward.

"After you."

Jeff smiled and moved past her. He fumbled with the flashlight, attempting to shove it through a belt loop in his jeans. It wouldn't fit and Megan rolled her eyes. She stepped up and took it from him, holding it comfortably in her left hand as she hefted the revolver in her right.

"I'll give it back whenever you need it," Megan reassured him.

Jeff nodded as he gripped the baseball bat more comfortably with both hands. The late afternoon sun beat down on them as they moved around to the back of the house. There was no fence so the trip took only a few seconds. He wiped the sweat from his brow and moved toward the patio. The sliding glass door was intact and a big couch with a love seat on top of it had been pushed against the doors. Jeff looked at the first floor windows and saw they were blacked out with what appeared to be garbage bags. No glass had been shattered. Backing up, he could see the second story windows had the shades pulled just like out front. Megan came around the corner and he gave her a thumbs-up before heading to the other side of the house.

The garage door was almost identical to the one Jeff had on his house: beige painted aluminum. The only difference was the two windows on it, while his had none. Black garbage bags covered them as well. He checked the handle on the garage door, twisting it quietly. It was locked. He tapped the bat against the window pane gently and it sounded normal. There was nothing behind the garbage bag to prevent the glass from being smashed in.

"You gonna break it?" Jeff nearly jumped out of his skin when Megan's question came from directly behind him.

"Jesus, woman!" he said to her as he grabbed at his chest. Megan's face split into a grin despite Jeff's obvious irritation.

"Sorry," was all she said without a speck of sincerity. After a moment he had to smile too. He made an exaggerated gesture like he was going to club her with the bat and they laughed together. Jeff shook his head and moved to the front of the house with Megan following. He walked to the front door and tried the knob. Two quick twists and he dropped his hand.

"Why don't you just ring the door bell?"

Jeff glanced over at Megan and she explained. "I mean, what difference does it make? You can't hear it out here. Look around you," she waved the gun at their deathly silent surroundings. "We have been talking out loud and driving the van and no one has noticed."

She had a point. Jeff nodded.

"Here goes nothing."

He pressed the button. Expecting to hear chimes, he was surprised when there was nothing. Megan leaned forward and pushed the button as well, repeatedly.

"Come on," she said, irritated and Jeff began to laugh quietly. She looked at him.

"Boy aren't we a pair?" Megan continued to stare at Jeff quizzically after his comment. "Did we think all the sudden that the electricity had come back on?" She sighed and shook her head, feeling stupid.

"Ding dong, dumb asses calling," she said and barked out a short self-deprecating laugh.

"Well, how about we just knock?" Jeff banged on the door. The silent response was deafening.

"Maybe they're upstairs sleeping." He looked skeptical at Megan's suggestion but rapped the edge of the door again, harder this time. The door frame rattled under the blows. Megan looked nervously up and down the street but saw the sound wasn't drawing any undue attention.

Jeff motioned for her to step back. He wound up and took a full swing at the glass with the bat. A spider web appeared in it but the ornate decorative display glass had lines of metal running through it. It would take several blows to knock it out.

"The side door would probably be a better bet," was all Megan said as he took another swing. Jeff ignored her and took several more swings before he paused, staring at the glass which was cracked but still in place.

"Fuck it," Jeff grumbled as he moved back to the side of the house. Megan hid her smile as she followed. He had already rammed the bat through one of the glass panels on the side door, shattering it, by the time she got there. "Nothing behind it," he commented, sticking the bat through the hole to lift the garbage bag and get a view inside. He motioned for her to hand him the flashlight.

Clicking it on, he swept it across the garage floor. Satisfied, Jeff set the bat down and reached inside for the deadbolt. It clicked open and they walked in.

The garage was jammed full of stacks of junk and an old Pontiac sedan. There were bags of clothes and several pieces of broken furniture. The claw hammer lying on top of one of the disassembled chairs led Jeff to believe that the wood was what the family had used in their effort to barricade the place.

His eyes narrowed as he stared past the piles of clothes and wood. It appeared that no one had broken into the place before them and yet no one had responded to all the noise they had made. The place smelled musty but that was a major improvement over the charnel house smell of the rest of the neighborhood.

Testing the knob, Jeff was surprised to find the interior door unlocked. He opened it a crack and nudged the flashlight against it. Megan tensed and held the revolver with both hands. When nothing happened, she relaxed slightly but kept a tight grip on the gun.

They moved inside. Particles of dust danced in the flashlight's beam as Jeff surveyed the kitchen. Splashing light in the shadows and listening for any movement, they moved across the floor carefully. The kitchen and family room was one large room, giving the two of them a clear view across the house. Splinters of light filtered in through the gaps in the couch barricade at the back door. Other windows had the ubiquitous black bags taped over them but whoever had done it had not done the best job and there was enough light trickling in that Jeff could turn off the flashlight as he stepped into the family room.

Megan noticed a pile of empty cans and cereal boxes stacked in and around the trash can in the kitchen and pointed it out to Jeff. He nodded. Someone had been staying here and from the looks of things had remained for quite some time. Other debris, including empty milk jugs, were scattered across the floor. A quick search of the pantry and kitchen cabinets revealed no more traces of food...at least anything edible.

The garage had been musty but the air inside the house was a bit riper. Jeff could smell the familiar stench of defecation that tended to overwhelm everything else once the toilets stopped working and there was no way to get rid of the human waste.

He was looking at the dual staircase leading down to the basement and up to the second floor when he heard a door creak open behind him and a sudden gagging noise.

Turning quickly, he saw Megan running to the kitchen sink. As he rushed to see what had happened he was hit by a wall of foulness that nearly knocked him over. Pulling up his sweatshirt, he covered his nose and mouth, but the rich smell of feces was overpowering. As Megan began to wretch into the sink he turned and discovered the source of this new and far more potent odor.

Shaking his head, Jeff pushed the bathroom door shut. He did not bother looking inside but could guess that there were buckets or other similar containers filled with piss and shit. Looking down, he saw the towel that had acted like the seal to keep as much of the smell inside the bathroom as possible.

Jeff waited patiently as Megan finished dry heaving.

With the door shut and the towel in place, the smell was shifting from overwhelming to barely tolerable once again. She wiped the thin line of spittle from her mouth and stood leaning over the sink.

"Go back outside. I can do this by myself," Jeff attempted to comfort her. "There isn't anyone here. They must have taken off." She shook her head but looked woozy and her knees almost gave out on her.

"Well, at least stay down here. I can't have you barfing up a lung while I check things out upstairs." Megan tried to retort but the heaves came back in a rush as she bent over the sink again. "I'll be back in a few minutes," Jeff said as she waved him off. He started toward the stairs.

It was gloomy on the second floor but even with the blinds and curtains closed there was more than enough light for him to see nothing was hiding in the shadows cast in the hallway. The sun was dipping into the west but it was still light outside. Setting the flashlight down at the top of the steps, he glanced over at the open area to the right. It was sparsely furnished with a small bookshelf, TV, and a couple of chairs. Looking down the hall, he could see that all the doors were shut. Moving into the sitting room, he opened the blinds on the window, letting in more light. With bat in hand, he turned to check out the bedrooms.

The smell wasn't nearly as strong up here and Jeff was already envisioning being able to bunk in for the night in one of the bedrooms. They could discuss plans for tomorrow after they settled in.

Moving across to the first door, he leaned against it and listened as he held the knob. As he had suspected, there was no sound except his own heartbeat. Still holding the bat, Jeff opened the door in a rush.

Nothing stirred and he moved in slowly, the bat held in front of him like a sword. The dim light revealed the room had been a teenage girl's. A couple of posters of the boy bands du jour and pink paint made it obvious. The bed was even made. It looked organized but a thick coating of dust made it clear it had not been used in quite some time.

He moved across the hall and checked the next room. This was a boy's. There was a NASCAR poster with some driver Jeff didn't recognize on the wall and several other posters with muscle bound superheroes on them. "Where were you guys when we needed you?" he whispered before stepping back into the hall.

The next room was another boy's, this one the younger of the two. Jeff smiled as he looked at the toys strewn across the room and the stickers adorning the walls. Unlike the others, this room had a lived in look about it, with books and stuffed animals lumped in random piles. He ran his finger over the top of the boy's dresser and it came away with as much dust as there had been in the other bedrooms.

Stepping back out into the hall he shut the door behind him. There were two more doors to check and he already knew which one was the bathroom. Although he could detect no odor coming from it, he was inclined to leave it shut after Megan's foul mistake downstairs.

The final room at the end of the hall had to be the master bedroom. This house was similar enough to Jeff's that it seemed obvious. Turning the knob, he pushed the door open.

He blinked as he looked in the room. What he saw was something out of his worst nightmare.

There were body parts splattered across the floor. The king sized bed looked as if someone had been taken apart piece by piece on top of it, with the remains spread from the head board down to the foot of the mattress.

Ragged piles of bones were strewn across the room. Something that looked like a child's rib cage lay crushed near a dresser, a trail of viscera leading from it to the back wall, which appeared to have an explosion of blood and entrails on it.

Drag marks around the room and smaller bones hinted at some sort of struggle having taken place. There were also other things that Jeff saw...lumps of pulped meat, gristle, and cartilage. It was a slaughterhouse.

But that was not the worst of it. Not by far.

Jeff's eyes focused on a woman's corpse partially hidden behind the king sized bed. He could see that it had not been long since she had been killed. In fact, the smells in the room were fresh; everyone in it had died recently.

The woman's body had been brutalized to the point where there was barely anything left of her neck or upper torso. Even her skull had been cracked into and her brains, or what remained of them, were dripping onto the floor.

When Jeff spotted her, horror blazed through him like an inferno, burning every nerve ending in his body. Her arms were outstretched toward him, her fingers gripping the carpet as if she had been trying to drag herself toward the door. Although the back of her skull was crushed her eyes remained open and it appeared as if she was staring at Jeff, a permanent scream frozen on her face.

When the corpse violently twitched, he took an involuntary step back and jammed his fist into his mouth to prevent a scream from bursting from his lips. A small yip still came out as his eyes grew wide in terror.

That was when a man stood up from behind the bed. He had been feasting on the lower half of her body and had been hidden from view. It was hard to believe that he wasn't visible before, as big as he was. Strings of his wife's intestines dangled from his mouth and a smear of blood covered the bottom half of his face.

The man's milky eyes widened when he saw Jeff and he let out a blood curdling scream as he charged. He was a blur as he tore across the room. Jeff had never seen someone infected move that fast.

He barely had time to react before the hulking figure crashed into him, driving him back into the hall and down to the floor. Jeff's breath came out in a huff and the baseball bat flew clear as his hand slammed into the wall.

"Fuck! Fuck! Fuck!" Jeff attempted to blurt out as the stench hit him and the tremendous weight of the man who had to be at least three hundred pounds came crashing down. The survivor's lungs were on fire and the words came out as a series of croaks. The infected man was a giant. Jeff moved his stinging hand and desperately beat at the ghoul's face. Its mouth was already plunging toward his shoulder, the cracked and broken teeth on display as the beast ignored his blows. Shifting his assault, Jeff pressed up against its forehead, hoping to keep the teeth at bay. The skin was dry and loose under his hand and he felt more than heard it starting to tear away from the man's scalp. Jeff knew if he tried to hold on for very long the flesh from the top of the ogre's head would slide off the skull and it wouldn't even notice.

Jeff felt a mammoth hand wrap around his throat and was able to suck in one last breath before his airway began to constrict. The man-mountain's fingers were trying to dig into the soft flesh there. As he fought to free himself Jeff knew it would not be long before his throat was ripped out.

He snatched at the monster's paw with his free hand as panic began kicking in. He was still holding the ghoul's head away but only had a few seconds to work with. He grabbed at the fingers around his throat and tried to pry them free. The skin was loose like on the forehead and there was no way to get a solid grip. Instead, Jeff was only peeling away layers of flesh as he frantically dug at the digits.

Despite the panicked kicks and the frenetic contortions of his body as he tried to throw the giant off, there was little Jeff could do as spots began to swim before his eyes. He realized he was about to pass out and felt his head starting to swim as his vision faded. All he could do was pray for unconsciousness before the teeth tore into his flesh.

There was a deafening roar in Jeff's ears and suddenly the grip loosened around his throat. There was a trickle of something dripping on his hand that had held the monstrosity's head up. It was running down his arm in thick globs. He struggled to breathe as he frantically fought to get the dead weight off of him. Pushing the head aside, Jeff moved the hand that had nearly crushed his neck away as he desperately sucked in air. Megan's face swam into view. She was saying something but he couldn't hear her. She looked alarmed as she tried helping him move the ton of dead flesh off his body.

It was not until Jeff could refill his lungs that he was able to help her shift the man's weight to the side and squirm free. He scuttled down the hall, backpedaling as fast as he could away from the giant carcass. He noticed the viscous fluid that had dripped down his arm looked like some sort of swamp mud. Jeff frantically started rubbing it on the carpet, desperate to get it off his skin.

Megan kneeled down in front of him, the revolver in her hand as she continued opening her mouth, but no sounds were coming out. She shook Jeff by the shoulders and looked as stunned as he felt. He grabbed her and pulled her close, hugging her. He didn't know what else to do to get her to stop.

They held each other for the next few minutes, their hearts finally slowing to a normal rate as they rocked back and forth, eyes closed. Jeff's breathing returned to normal although his throat was throbbing and he had to keep his breathing shallow to avoid sharp pains.

When he let Megan go it dawned on him that he had briefly gone deaf. Now a ringing in Jeff's ears was signifying the return of his hearing, along with the buzzing that was Megan's voice. After another minute he was able to comprehend what she had been trying to say to him.

"...thought he had gotten you...sorry that I had to do that, but there was..." It was still choppy but Jeff nodded at her and gave her a shaky smile.

"You did great," he heard himself say as he continued to lean against the wall. He closed his eyes in an attempt to get his bearings but still felt dizzy. A whopper of a headache was also announcing its arrival. Jeff opened his eyes again so he could regain his balance.

He tried to stand and nearly slid back down the wall.

Waving Megan off as she moved in to help, he got it on the second attempt. Looking down at a huge lump of decayed flesh at his feet, Jeff shook his head. None of them had moved that fast before. Outside of the fact that its brains were now dripping in thick chunks down the wall, the ghoul looked to be in pretty good shape. Decomposition, which was so common amongst the infected, was limited. In fact, outside of the dry, leathery skin, the man looked almost normal.

Jeff looked at Megan. Despite their little close encounter she looked better than how he had left her downstairs. Grinning, he chucked her lightly on the shoulder. She blushed and smiled meekly.

Suddenly, her eyes went wide, as if she had just remembered something. Raising the revolver, she turned to face the master bedroom. "Are there any more of them?"

Megan began moving toward the door and Jeff yelled out as he ran ahead of her. "No!"

He blocked her path and without looking into the room he pulled the door shut. "You don't want to go in there. Trust me."

Jeff held his arms out, guarding the door. Megan was startled by his reaction but saw the look on his face and slowly nodded as she lowered the gun. Jeff's shoulders sagged in relief as he moved back toward her.

"I'm sorry," he apologized as he put his arm around her shoulder, turning her around. "But there's nothing in there you need to see."

Megan looked up at Jeff but he kept his eyes forward as they moved back down the hall. Less than a minute later they were outside, climbing back into the van. As they pulled away from the curb, Jeff never looked back at the house as he rubbed gently at his bruised throat.

Fifteen minutes later they found another house. The garage was open and there were no boarded up windows, which Jeff hoped indicated that the owners had fled long ago.

A quick but far more thorough search confirmed the

house was indeed abandoned. Whoever had lived there had left in a rush, like so many other families that had chosen to either head to one of the emergency shelters hastily set up by the National Guard or anywhere they thought they could go to escape the ravages of the virus that had burned through the earth's population in a matter of days.

Jeff pulled the van into the garage. Megan was already inside searching for anything they could add to their meager food supplies.

He stepped out of the vehicle and moved toward the driveway. Scanning the street, he saw nothing that caught his eye except for the sun, which was beginning to set. Houses cast long shadows as the bright yellow orb continued to sink below the horizon. Off in the distance, a few blocks away, he could see wisps of smoke curling up to the sky from the smoldering ruins of his house.

Jeff rubbed his eyes. His headache was in full bloom and it felt as if his brain was trying to pound its way out of his skull. In a way, it was a comfort...a distraction from the real pain he was feeling.

Taking one last look around, he began pulling the garage door closed. He wondered if there was any booze in the house, because all he wanted to do was drink until he forgot everything that had happened that day.

Chapter 13

"We need to get going."

Jeff rubbed his eyes and sat up. Sunlight trickled in through the drawn curtains, spreading fingers of light across the floor and onto the bed. There had been no alcohol in the house, but he still felt hung over as he ran his tongue over his teeth. His mouth tasted like a baby dragon had peed in it.

Megan was standing at the foot of the bed, wearing a clean sweatshirt and jeans. They were loose on her, but given her near anorexic condition, Jeff thought they were a pretty good fit. She looked freshly scrubbed and there was something about her that he could not pinpoint, but she looked sharper, more alert, than she had the day before.

He nodded as he ran his fingers through his tangled hair.

"There are plenty of clothes that might fit you in the closet," Megan said and Jeff looked down at his sweatshirt and jeans, which he had slept in. They were in bad shape. Besides being drenched in sweat, there were splatters of dry blood and dirt smeared all over them. "I put a couple of bottles of water in the bathroom from the ones we found downstairs..." She let the comment hang in the air.

"I know I smell like an outhouse," Jeff cracked a smile. "I'll change and clean up."

A small grin passed over Megan's lips. "I'm going downstairs to see what else we can take with us." She paused, looking at her hands and picking at a fingernail. Jeff stared, waiting for her to say whatever was bothering her.

"We *are* going to leave, right?"

Jeff sighed as he stretched, rubbing the bruise on his neck self-consciously. It was a garish purple but didn't feel as bad as it looked. He recalled their conversation from the night before and understood why Megan was acting so timidly.

They had argued about leaving immediately. Jeff thought it might be a good idea to stick it out for a few days while she wanted to figure out a way around the blockade of cars so they could start trying to find other survivors. She suggested checking out the emergency shelters and when Jeff laughed bitterly she glared at him until he fumbled over an apology and mumbled an excuse, saying *"you never know"* to placate her.

In the end, they had agreed to wait until morning to decide. Megan fell asleep as soon as her head hit the pillow but Jeff was stuck tossing and turning over the next few hours as he tried to figure out what they hell they were going to do.

He nodded, too tired and feeling far too shitty to argue again. Megan's smile lit up her face.

"Great!" She turned to leave the room. "I'll see if I can rustle up some breakfast."

"I'll take two eggs over easy, three slices of bacon, toast with just a touch of butter...and a gallon of coffee," Jeff said as he stared at the floor between his legs and tried to keep from throwing up on his shoes.

He heard Megan's laugh as she walked down the hall. It sounded happy. "I'll see what I can do."

Five minutes later he felt well enough to stand up and make his way to the bathroom. He saw the bottled water Megan had brought up, along with a bar of soap and some toothpaste. Shaking his head, Jeff laughed and stared at the mirror.

It was hard to believe the person looking back at him was Jeffery Blaine. The grey streaks in his scraggly beard and the drawn and haggard expression made him feel a couple of decades older than his thirty five years. His hair was a tangled, curly mess and hung in greasy clumps around his face.

He flashed a peace sign at the mirror along with his best stoner pose. "Dirty fucking hippie," he mumbled under his breath. He thought if he could find a pair of Birkenstocks in the closet it would complete the look.

Stripping, Jeff began splashing water on his face and body, unconcerned with the mess he was making since they were leaving anyway.

A few minutes later, after having found a pair of jeans and a sweatshirt that fit reasonably well, Jeff felt like a new man. The headache had subsided and the scent of soap on his skin smelled good. When he walked down the steps he was actually cheerful.

When he hit the first floor he spotted Megan sitting at the kitchen table. She was facing away from him.

"Where's my breakfast, woman?" He said, lowering his voice with exaggerated irritation.

When Megan ignored the snarky comment Jeff shrugged. He moved into the kitchen. "I guess I'll just have to fix it myself." He shook his head. "I can't believe you're already shirking your womanly duties."

He began looking through the cabinets. There was no food, though there were plenty of baking supplies. "Hey Megan, you could bake me a cake. That might make up for no eggs and bacon laid out for breakfast."

He smiled and turned to her, wondering why Megan wasn't laughing or tossing off a snide riposte. When Jeff saw that she was staring off into space he moved slowly toward her.

"Hello?" He snapped his fingers and waved his hand in front of her eyes. "Anyone home?" Megan finally looked at him. His demeanor immediately changed from slightly annoyed to concern.

"Megan?"

"They're back." Her voice was subdued.

Jeff stared at her for a moment before moving toward one of the windows at the front of the house. Carefully bending the blinds to peak out, he scanned the street as he heard Megan's voice drift over to him.

"I wanted to see what the weather was like. I opened the front door and saw one of them. It was about a block away. I don't think it saw me, but then I saw another moving around across the street. I went to shut the door and...there was another. I'm not sure, maybe there were more..." her voice trailed off, the monotone account becoming background noise as Jeff searched the street. He began counting the stiffs he saw on his fingers and had to stop when he realized there were too many.

Megan was staring at him as he came walking back to the kitchen. The spark he had seen in her eyes just a little while ago had dimmed but Jeff could still see both the hope and fear in them that had always been there. Any thoughts of renewing their argument about sticking around the neighborhood vanished completely.

Jeff forced a smile to his lips as he spoke. "Grab everything you can. Let's get the hell out of here."

Chapter 14

It had been a busy intersection at one time but had fallen silent over the past few weeks. The fires had long since died out and only charred residue remained. Destruction ran in random patterns; one building wiped out while the one next door left undamaged.

A Dodge Intrepid teetered precariously on a brick wall at the entrance of a convenience mart. Wind made it creak and sway on its perch. The store shelves beyond the wreck were ransacked. A few items remained but everything of any value had been cleared out.

The *Quick-n-Go* across the street was in far worse condition. Two of its gas pumps had been sheared off at their base. The burnt out husk of a vehicle responsible for the damage had come to a crunching stop at a concrete barrier housing a dumpster on the back side of the parking lot. One of its tires had blown out before it connected with the pumps as it jumped a ditch. Sparks from the undercarriage ignited both the pumps and the gas tank on the vehicle. The resulting explosion sent the corrugated metal roof above crashing down, where it slammed into several cars parked underneath, crushing them and the people inside. Billowing flames from the two squashed pumps caused a chain reaction and the rest of the pumps erupted into fireballs as well.

All that remained was a few burnt out vehicles and bits of human remains baked into the cement. The corpses were seared carrion for scavengers to pick over. The building's contents was annihilated by the heat and pressure of the explosions. Glass and metal superheated and fused together and the ceiling tiles collapsed on top of the mess, bubbling as they melted and turned into a black ash that created a fine patina over the entire mess. The outer frame of the building was all that remained standing and looked like a charred skeleton of some giant beast.

The drug store diagonal to the *Quick-n-Go* was mostly intact even though heaps of trash and blistered vehicles populated its parking lot. The building still looked new. It was made almost entirely of stone with a few faux windows running along its side. Only at the entrance facing the intersection was there any building materials besides granite. The glass doors were shattered though the surrounding entryway, also made of glass, was still intact. The metal door frames were bent and pressed inward and small pebbles of glass lay scattered across the tile floor. The small metal racks that once held Auto Trader and real estate magazines were crushed flat on the floor and there was shredded paper strewn throughout the vestibule with bloody footprints splattered on them.

A ladder truck from the Milfield Fire Department was in the intersection along with an army vehicle known as a deuce and a half. There were also several local township police cruisers and a camouflaged Humvee with a Squad Automatic Weapon, or SAW, mounted on the roof. They had been parked around the exterior of the intersection, forming a barrier to traffic coming from all directions. An ambulance stood sentry inside the jury rigged stronghold, its rear door hanging open with the remnants of medical supplies scattered on the ground, smashed and useless. The vehicles were all wrecks, torn and shattered. There were dents and scratches, flattened tires and burst gas tanks. Expended weapon cartridges lay scattered across the pavement by the hundreds.

Above the vehicles a cable holding up the traffic signal

units had snapped and they had crashed into the fire truck. Shards of red, amber, and green glass lay scattered across the roadway. The culprit was a car that had slammed into a light pole at one of the corners. The pole had collapsed into the parking lot of a pizza delivery joint. A rusted out old Cadillac was now resting on top of the pole, its front tires slightly off the ground. Its windshield showed where the driver's head made contact. There was a spider web of cracks radiating outward from the blood soaked spot on the glass.

Scavengers had picked most of the scattered bones clean and even the remnants of blood and tattered clothing had been washed away by rain or blown away in the wind. The sun baked the rest of the gore into the pavement but the area had been cleansed of most signs of the former human inhabitants. The area was a dead zone.

In the distance something shattered the persistent silence.

It was a car engine, its roar reverberating off the buildings as it gunned and hesitated repeatedly. It grew louder and quieter in turn, the noise coming and going at random intervals.

The roads surrounding the intersection were clogged with stalled and demolished vehicles. It was a maze that would challenge any driver to navigate even at a snail's pace.

Jeff and Megan found freedom from their residential prison by plowing through several fenced in yards at the edge of the subdivision and avoiding the vehicle blockade entirely. Their journey of less than a couple of miles afterward took thirty minutes and gave them a bitter taste of what the outside world now had to offer.

Most of the vehicles they came across were abandoned, with doors wide open and discarded suitcases strewn across the pavement. Others were smashed into, telltale drag marks and trails of blood the only evidence as to what had happened to the owners. But some of the cars still had bodies inside.

The corpses of the people who managed to stay locked in their vehicles were in bad shape. A month of summer heat and direct sunlight had taken its toll, bloating and warping them until they were unrecognizable. In some cases, the bodies had exploded and splattered their rotten contents on windows, hiding the most gruesome aspects of their demise.

But the worst was the little girl.

She was locked in a car seat in the back of an Altima on the side of the road. At first Jeff thought she was just like the rest of the corpses until he saw her arm twitch. As he looked closer her eyes opened. When she twisted around to look at him Jeff nearly screamed. Her skin had gone runny, having melted away from her face and arms in thick, gluey globs. The blistered remains of her visage made her eyes look wide and haunted and her grin demonic. As Jeff drove on he couldn't be sure if Megan saw the girl because she never said a word.

The blue minivan made agonizingly slow progress toward the intersection, braking then shifting into reverse on several occasions as it moved past one obstacle or backed up and circled another. A few solitary plague-ravaged people limped into view from the houses and wooded areas surrounding the road but were scattered and could not keep up with the van, even at its creeping pace. When the Odyssey finally came to a halt a hundred yards from the intersection, Jeff and Megan paused to survey the destruction.

"I think the junior high was one of those emergency shelters the National Guard opened up," Megan said as they stared at the clog of military and police vehicles up ahead.

After a few moments of silence she looked at Jeff and realized he hadn't heard her, or wasn't paying attention. She nudged him with her elbow.

"Huh? Oh, sorry. I was just..." Jeff waved his hand in front of them, showing a trace of the shock Megan knew was on her face as well.

"I know. It's hard to believe." She looked back

outside, trying to grasp what had become of all the shops and stores she remembered so well from her three years living in the area. Megan blotted the thoughts out as she tried to focus. "I think we should check out the Junior High."

Jeff slowly looked off into the distance in the direction of the high school and junior high. He shook his head. "I don't think that's such a good idea."

He pointed above the buildings that lined the street. "See that? That smoke? I don't like the looks of it."

Megan scrunched up her face until she caught sight of the smoke curling toward the sky. She leaned forward and shook her head slowly.

"I think that's too far away. It's coming from the city or at least a suburb closer to it than Milfield. The junior high is just a mile down the road."

Jeff did not respond immediately. He studied the fire truck and other vehicles at the intersection. His eyes narrowed with understanding and he turned to Megan.

"I *really* don't think we should go that way." He raised his hand to stall her protest and pointed to the vehicles in front of them. "See that fire truck?"

Megan gave him an irritated look telling him how stupid she thought his question was.

"I mean: so you see how it's set up?" Jeff paused as she looked out at the truck once again and waited until she nodded. "I think there was some sort of last stand here."

He let his words sink in as they both studied the fire truck. It was blocking the road leading to the junior high and beyond, where the interstate that circled Cincinnati was. Downtown was a mere twenty-five miles from where they sat.

Megan's face was a picture of conflicting emotions as she let the ramifications of Jeff's words sink in. The city was ground zero for the first viral outbreaks in the region. From there it spiraled outward, attacking the suburban landscape in random spots as it built momentum and grew out of the control of civil and military authorities trying to contain its progress.

Jeff could see the sparkle of tears in Megan's eyes even as she tried to blink them away. His heart sank as he watched her struggle with the reality that it was unlikely anyone they knew was a survivor. The shelter had, in all probability, been overrun weeks ago.

He sat in silence, unsure of what to say that might offer her comfort. As he stared down at the steering wheel he tried to clear his mind and focus on the magnitude of what they were facing.

"So where do we go from here?"

Jeff glanced over at Megan but she was still looking down the road. She rubbed at her eyes fiercely with the back of her hand and sniffled but otherwise showed no further emotion as she asked the question.

"I think we should head out into the country. We might have a fighting chance out there," He suggested without hesitation. They needed to get as far away from the city as possible.

"Yah," Megan whispered and sniffled again. After a moment she grimaced and shook her head. "Probably a bunch of gun nuts and survivalists out there, but what other choice do we have?"

Jeff shrugged. "Maybe, but they're the ones who have the best shot of making it through something like this...not a couple of suburban dip wads like us."

Megan tilted her head and stared at him. She could see a gleam in his eyes as he winked at her. She gave him a half-hearted laugh in response.

"Okay then, Mister Dip Wad, let's get the hell out of here."

Jeff grinned, relieved that Megan seemed to be handling things well enough to toss a bit of abuse his way.

Lifting his foot off the break, he let the van roll forward slowly and scanned the immediate buildings. They had been sitting near the intersection for a couple of minutes and had seen no movement thus far. As his eyes moved from building to building, they landed on the drug store and stayed on it for several seconds. A look of grim concentration came over Jeff's face.

"What?" Megan asked as they slowed to a stop again. She looked at him and then swiveled around to see what he was staring at with such intensity. She stiffened, fearing an attack. When all she saw was the drug store and not much else she relaxed slightly and turned back to Jeff to await his explanation.

"I think..." he paused and then, nodding vigorously, seemed to confirm something with himself. "Yep, definitely."

"What, for chrissakes?" Megan blurted out.

Jeff snorted at the frustration in his companion's voice. He nodded at the drug store.

"Before we go, I think we should do a little shopping."

Chapter 15

Jeff was grateful for the sunlight that crept inside the entrance to the drug store, even though much of it was blotted out by the minivan, which was parked directly in front of the demolished front doors, blocking anything from getting past it from outside. Unfortunately, the light only illuminated a short distance into the building. The store was cavernous and he could see another glimmer of light at the back, where the pharmacy drive through window was, but much of the middle of the store was buried in a deep layer of darkness.

He gave one look back toward the van where Megan sat behind the wheel and sighed. It had taken some work convincing her to let him check out the drug store but in the end she had agreed, knowing just as well as he did that they desperately needed supplies. She still refused to come inside, stating that he might be crazy but she wasn't. Megan had gone so far as to give him ten minutes to get back to the van before she would leave without him. He thought she was joking until he saw the naked fear in her eyes. That was when he nodded and promised to be quick.

Most of the aisles were still standing, although much of the contents was scattered on the floor. Makeup, candy, and over-priced DVDs covered the ground and had been trampled repeatedly. Jeff turned on the flashlight and swung it back and forth. To his left were the registers and photo development area. Much of the product hanging on the walls-film, batteries, more candy, magazines...was still there, untouched. As he crept further into the store the rubber soles of his hiking boots squeaked as he skirted the piles of trash on the floor.

He noticed congealed blood pooled between several aisles. Down one lane it looked like a skirmish had occurred, with a jumble of bloody footprints layered on top of one another and thick ropy splatters of red sprayed against a display of vacuum cleaner bags and humidifiers. Several shelves had collapsed in the area.

Jeff tried to detect any sounds that might hint of anyone still in residence in the drug store but could hear nothing except his own breathing. Gritting his teeth, he moved deeper into the gloom.

He found an overturned shopping cart and righted it. Pushing it along, he moved through the aisles that did not have most of their contents on the floor and started grabbing anything that looked even remotely useful. Product was sparse but there was enough remaining that he rubbed his hands in glee.

Jeff grabbed bandages, aspirin, allergy medicine, deodorant, hydrogen peroxide, razors, shaving cream, tampons (stifling a giggle as he did), and anything else within reach. He filled the metal cart and built up speed, the flashlight jammed in an arm pit as he grabbed snacks and cases of soda. Unfortunately there was no food more substantial than that but he knew they had already collected quite a few canned goods from the house they had hidden in the night before.

He glanced at his watch: three more minutes before Megan started freaking out. He was staring at the timepiece when the contents of a shelf next to his head crashed down on him.

The flashlight clattered to the floor as Jeff let out an involuntary squeal and dove forward. He thought he felt a hand touching his shoulder as several bags of chips and boxes of cookies fell on him. He could not see anything as he slammed into another shelf and nearly sent it teetering over. Instead, he tripped on something between his feet and sprawled headlong, landing on palms and knees as he slid across the floor.

Quickly rolling over, he scooted backwards in a crab like fashion, trying to get a fix on where he was. The flashlight was still rolling and its light pointing away. Jeff moved his hand back and forth across the floor until he found a small cardboard box. He grabbed it, cocking his arm back, ready to launch it at anything that came forward in the darkness.

He could hear something over the pounding of blood in his ears, but barely. It sounded like scurrying and scratching. Although there was no moaning, Jeff had learned not to rely on that as the only indicator he was in the presence of a predator.

His pupil's dilated as he absorbed all the dim light available and looked out in front of him. He tried to scan for any looming shapes and saw none. After another thirty seconds to give his breathing a chance to return to normal he quietly stood and moved back to the shopping cart and fallen flashlight. Picking it up, he pointed it toward the shelf.

It only took a few moments to discover the culprit. Jeff smiled in spite of himself as he saw several shredded Fritos bags with small teeth marks on them. The marks had been made by some kind of rodent. A rat or perhaps a squirrel had taken up residence in the abandoned store. Shaking his head, he took a deep breath, trying to throttle back on the adrenaline. Gripping the shopping cart, he headed toward the pharmacy counter.

After a quick leap over the counter he was scanning the medications. It took a minute or so to find some of the drugs he knew would be useful. Grabbing as much as he could carry, he tossed pill bottles over the counter at the cart. When he cleared out as much as he could, he launched himself back over the counter. Staring at the filled cart, Jeff was about to head back to the front when he noticed more bloody foot prints off to his left. They led to a swinging door marked *Employees Only*. It was next to the pharmacy and probably led back to the store's stock room. He recalled a door outside near the drive-through that must have served as a loading dock.

The debate in his head on whether he should risk taking a look lasted a scant two seconds. Leaving the cart, Jeff moved to the door. Flipping off the flashlight, he stood and listened.

He held the flashlight like a club but doubted anyone was back there. They would have responded to all the noise his clumsy fall had caused. Then he remembered the menacing giant from the day before. The creature had been far too busy disemboweling his wife to give a damn about any distant noises. Jeff tensed but did not move away from the door. He knew he wasn't prepared but felt compelled to take a look anyway.

Listening for another few seconds, he began to hear a low humming noise. It sounded like a machine-maybe a generator or refrigerator. Staying to the side of the door, Jeff used the long barrel of the flashlight to push it open. When nothing burst through, he moved in front of the doorway to look inside.

The stench pounced, as if it had been waiting for a victim to assault. It was overwhelming. The combination of heat and a small sealed place made Jeff feel like he had stepped into a crematorium basement where the furnace was kept burning day and night.

It was the stock room, as he had guessed. There were racks reaching to the ceiling filled with boxes of various shapes and sizes. The ones higher up had avoided the spray of blood but those closer to the floor were saturated.

A cloud of flies rose angrily from their meal, angry at being disturbed. There were more of them than Jeff had ever seen in his life. They were making the furious humming noise. After a few seconds most of them settled down and got back to their meal, which consisted of blood and entrails splattered across the floor.

Jeff covered his mouth as he felt his gorge rising. He tried to steady himself as he saw the torn bodies scattered throughout the room. They were devastated, ripped to pieces, but...

Eyes scanning the carnage, he caught sight of what he had deduced was the reason these people had not succumbed to the virus. Next to a sprawled out appendage was a semi-automatic hand gun.

The people who hid in the store room had been mauled so thoroughly it was hard to tell where one body ended and another began but Jeff's best guess was that they had formed some sort of suicide pact. Someone had pulled the trigger and put bullets in each of their comrade's heads before turning the gun on themselves.

The gun was drenched with gore and he dismissed the idea of stepping over the slick remains to grab it. It was already enough of a challenge not letting go of the contents of his stomach as it was. Fighting against the feeling of helplessness and remorse that threatened to consume him, Jeff turned to leave.

As the metal door swung shut again he did not look back. He grabbed the shopping cart and began pushing it toward the dim light of the entrance.

Wiping the sweat off his face, he blinked and his teeth clenched as he fought to gain control over his anger. The world had become a madhouse-an endless supply of macabre images slowly eating away at his sanity, bit by bloody bit.

Jeff gripped the handle of the shopping cart tight. The anger and fear tickling the back of his mind began to subside as a crystal clear thought cut through all the crap floating around in his head: he wanted to live. That was all that mattered. He knew he was smarter than those things trying to kill him and there was no way, no how, he was going to end up like the poor saps whose guts were strewn across the storage room floor. A grim smile crossed his face as he rolled his cart through the aisles. In that instant he felt more confident than he had in weeks.

The smile faltered as Jeff got close to the entrance of the store and heard Megan screaming.

Chapter 16

Megan screamed again as the sliding door of the minivan opened. She turned, gun in hand, and suddenly Jeff was staring down the barrel of the .357 Magnum.

He raised his hands and yelled "Whoa, it's me! It's okay Megan, it's me!" He froze as he saw the fear in her eyes. For an instant he thought she was going to pull the trigger. Something like recognition passed over her face and Megan's hand dipped slightly, though she was still freaked out.

The sound of a fist slamming into one of the windows caused her to whip around toward the noise. Jeff looked as well and could see blood caking the rear window where the fist had connected.

He could also hear the moans. The van was surrounded. The infected had crept out of their various hiding places: abandoned cars, dark shadows, and from inside the other buildings where they had hidden from the blazing sun. That they had come for them did not surprise Jeff. What did surprise him was that Megan had not already started shooting.

He could see several figures through the dirty window glass moving slowly toward the minivan. Only a handful had reached the vehicle so far but they were a gruesome lot. One that had found its way to the driver's side window made Jeff squirm. Its face was obliterated with chunks of glass wedged into its sparse flesh. One eye was split in half, the largest shard of glass jammed deep within the orb. Its other eye stared at Megan balefully as it hissed with all its shattered teeth and blackened gums on display.

"We need to leave *now*, Jeff!" was all Megan could say as she kept turning in her chair and holding the gun in front of her, as if not quite sure which grisly monster to shoot at first. The van was starting to rock back and forth.

Jeff turned back toward the shopping cart and began grabbing armfuls of items out of it to toss into the van. "Help me with this shit and we'll get the hell out of here."

"Jeff...*please.*" He could hear the desperate pleading in her voice and knew Megan wasn't about to move out of the driver's seat. As she began repeating the word *please* over and over, her voice began to rise. Jeff's arms were a blur as he dug into the cart and tossed more of its content into the minivan. The thuds of fists were becoming more insistent, like the sound of a hailstorm. He didn't look up as he kept his hands moving from the cart to the van in rapid succession.

"JEFF. WE HAVE TO LEAVE RIGHT NOW!" Megan spit out the words as she grabbed the car key with shaking hands and attempted to turn it.

"Just one more second! I almost have everything!" Jeff grunted as he tried to grab a hold of more than his hands could manage. Cans and bags of chips spilled on to the ground as he shoveled what he could inside. A buzzing sound filled the air and the van jolted as the engine turned over. Jeff recognized the noise and saw the automatic door beginning to close. He also saw Megan fumbling with the gear shift.

Dropping what was left in his hands he dove through the closing door and heard the sound of metal on metal and squealing tires as the van shot away from the entrance of the drug store. Grabbing hold of an arm rest, Jeff held on tight as Megan whipped the Odyssey around the parking lot. There were several loud thumps as the infected were pushed out of the way. The minivan bounced erratically and then corrected, stable again on four wheels. At least one of the bodies had fallen in front of the vehicle and Megan did not stop as they rolled over it. The side door finally clicked shut and the buzzing noise disappeared.

Swinging the steering wheel side to side frantically, Megan avoided the larger clusters of bodies attempting to grab for them. Several more stiffs were knocked to the side as they swerved out of the parking lot, hitting the small ditch surrounding it and popping up onto the street. Everything Jeff had just tossed on the seats scattered to the floor and began rolling around the cargo area. He joined the supplies and landed ass-up on the floor. From his vantage point he could see nothing and had a hard time crawling back to a sitting position.

"Calm down Megan! We're gonna crash!" he tried to yell over the still squealing tires and revving engine. Jeff could not hear his own voice as he grabbed a hold of a chair to pull himself up. The van finally straightened out and the disheveled man was able to slide into the front passenger seat. He was barely settled when Megan slammed on the brakes, nearly sending him through the windshield.

"Enough!" Jeff yelled, this time loud enough for her to hear as she gunned the engine and wrenched the steering wheel around to weave in and out of the stationary traffic. Megan jumped slightly at the sound of his voice but her eyes did not move off the road. She slowed slightly but retained her death grip on the steering wheel as the van darted around stalled cars and lunging bodies. As they moved further away from the intersection the cars remained an issue but there were fewer ghouls to dodge.

"Ease up just a little bit," Jeff tried again as he put his hand on Megan's shoulder. She viciously shrugged it off and he acted as if she had slapped him, backing away slowly. "Okay, okay. Sorry." Looking down, he leaned over and picked up the .357, which had fallen to the floorboards.

"If NASCAR ever gets rolling again, I'll be sure to sign you up."

It did not elicit the smile Jeff had hoped for but the

intensity in Megan's eyes seemed to drop a notch. Holding the wheel steady she reached over and pulled her seatbelt on, which made him relax a bit more. Her driving was steadier as they weaved in out of the clog of vehicles and headed down the road. A random path of destruction continued from structure to structure but the vehicles were starting to thin out as the survivors moved on.

The duo was silent as Megan continued to dodge the occasional persistent plague victim. She clipped a couple at first but now the few figures on the road were getting easier to avoid.

The sloping hood of the van had several sizeable dents in it that were splattered with something that looked far too thick and runny to be blood. Jeff was staring at the new paint job when the minivan swerved again and he heard a muffled thud as another body went spinning off into a ditch, pirouetting as it got knocked away by the hit. He watched, fascinated by the creature's single moment of grace before it fell and disappeared from view.

"Sorry," Megan whispered as the asphalt beneath them started resembling a road again instead of a parking lot. Jeff cocked his head to the side, unsure of what he had heard.

"I'm sorry," the driver repeated, glancing at her passenger for a moment.

"Screw that. You did great," he smiled, relieved that the tension between them was broken. "I meant what I said: you drove this puppy like a pro. I would have probably smashed into one of those wrecks back there."

Megan didn't share the smile but her chest puffed up slightly. They sat in silence for the next few minutes, content to look out the windows. As the van crept along they saw fewer corpses, less of the infected, and a stretch of road with no more wrecks or abandoned vehicles.

"So?" Megan said after a while. She waited for Jeff to look at her before continuing. "Gallatin then?"

He nodded. Gallatin was due east and out toward the country. The town was a mirror image of Milfield except it was smaller and still held on to its rural roots. There were plenty of trailer parks, farms, and big undeveloped plots of land out that way.

Jeff stared out at the surrounding landscape, which looked deceptively normal. The woods were a bit thicker along the stretch of road they were driving and the houses more spread out. He knew that as long as he didn't look too close it was easy to pretend things were back to the way they had been before the virus paid the world a visit.

They went over a rise in the road and the daydream was shattered. The trees fell away and they were moving past another neighborhood no different from any of the others the two refugees had seen before. It was a mishmash of damaged properties and others left untouched. Several of the infected were milling about and turned to look as the vehicle rolled by. The sad wretches tried to follow but never got close as Jeff watched them disappeared in the rearview mirror.

He gave brief directions to Megan. They would take one of the lesser traveled routes with the hope that it would not be too congested with stalled traffic. It would lead them directly to Gallatin.

Jeff fiddled with the radio as they rolled along. He began with AM, pressing seek and letting it run through the static. It lapped the entire band with no results. He switched to FM and repeated the process. There was nothing, not even an automated emergency broadcast. Those messages had been looped to play over and over, non-stop, when all the live broadcasts had vanished. Even the recorded voices had disappeared off the airwaves.

Megan reached over to turn the radio off. Jeff had already sat back and was staring off into space when she did. He barely noticed when the hiss of static disappeared.

He snapped out of his trance a few minutes later when the car slowed and began turning left. The intersection was clear of traffic though several cars and eighteen wheelers sat on both sides of the road. There were huge crease marks on many of the vehicles, as if something like a bulldozer had pushed them out of the way. As he looked he spotted no heavy machinery in the area. There were a few sideways skid marks on the asphalt but no other hints as to what might have happened.

As they left the crossroad Jeff dismissed the damaged vehicles and their possible meaning from his mind. He closed his eyes and began to drift off. It felt like only a few seconds later when he heard the van slowing to a stop.

Lifting his head, he glanced at Megan and then looked out his window to see what she was staring at. He was about to shake his head and tell her it was a bad idea to stop there when he saw the expression on her face. He examined the building they were parked in front of a bit closer.

It was a small brick fronted church with a wooden sign out front. There was little ornamentation to the edifice itself. The roof was pointed and several long, narrow windows faced the road. A small indentation in the building served as the entryway, with its glass double-doors still intact.

Next to the doorway on the ground was the one thing that differentiated the church from all the others they had seen on their short journey. It was a tall wooden structure, nearly as high as the doors themselves. From a distance one might mistake it for a miniature steeple but the sign out front made it clear what this decorative feature was.

The wooden sign in front of the church was decorated with a circular graphic and Lighthouse Baptist Fellowship in bright yellow letters painted on a brown background. A picture of a sea cliff with a lighthouse shining down on a rocky shore was carved below the lettering. There was a space for the "Message of the week" underneath, which read: *Revelations 6:8 And behold, a pale horse, and he who sat on it, his name was Death. Hades followed with him. Authority over one fourth of the earth, to kill with the sword, with famine, with death, and by the wild animals of the earth was given to him.*

"Not very original," Jeff smirked as he scanned the commentary. Megan frowned but kept looking at the modest doors of the church. There was nothing grand about the place. No stained glass, no bell to summon the congregation, no statues of Jesus. Just a tidy little building with quite a few cars crammed into its small parking lot.

Jeff resisted saying anything else or asking questions. If Megan was saying a prayer for the dearly departed or reminiscing about the good old days, he could manage to keep his mouth shut while she did. He studied the church further and saw there were no signs of attack around the perimeter or in the parking lot. The area looked clear of bodies. Relaxing, he decided to sit and wait until Megan was ready to get rolling again.

The peaceful scene exploded less than a minute later when several gangrenous congregants burst through the doors of the church, slouching toward them. There was a sharp intake of breath to Jeff's left as it happened. He, on the other hand, felt surprisingly calm as more and more stiff forms poured out of the building. Most wore suits and what had once been pretty dresses before their owners started to bloat, leak, and weep caustic fluids.

The first woman out the door was gussied up in her Sunday best with several silk flowers still stuck in her wispy grey hair. Hair that now floated above her skull like writhing snakes. The flowers retained some of their faux beauty, though they were smudged and smeared with caked grease. Stripes of gore mixed with the soft silken white petals, which gave them a zebra-like appearance. She and those that followed limped toward the minivan over the burnt lawn of the church.

Jeff forced his eyes off the growing rabble and back toward Megan.

She was still looking toward the entrance, her eyes moist though she wasn't crying. He moved to block her view of the mass of corrupt forms moving toward them but Megan didn't even blink when he did.

When she spoke a moment later her voice sounded far off, distant.

"We were told it would be safe here. They said we should come with them. Why did this happen? I don't understand."

"They were infected like everyone else."

The bitter words caught Megan's attention and her eyes refocused on Jeff. She looked angry but also fractured and unsure of herself.

"God couldn't protect them Megan. No one could. If you had come here with them you would have been infected too, no matter how hard you prayed."

Jeff started to see the cold fire in Megan's eyes that he had seen before. He wanted to shrink back but something inside compelled him to push harder.

"God helps those who help themselves." He jerked his head backwards, not daring to look at the onrush of bodies. "They were lambs led to the slaughter. Hell, it doesn't even look like they barred the doors. They probably just kept on praying and thought the rapture was coming."

Megan's face went nuclear. "You cold hearted bastard! I had friends in there, not that you give a shit!"

Jeff returned the angry look, his peppered with frustration. "Megan, it doesn't *matter* if I care! What difference would it make if I said I was sorry they were infected?" He paused, but realized he had already said too much. Regret surfaced on his face and then shifted back to anger to hide his embarrassment. "I AM sorry, okay!? Does that make you feel any better?"

Megan's expression didn't change. Jeff tried to collect himself and calm down as he heard the moans getting closer. He took a deep breath and reached out to touch her. Megan shrunk away, her expression appalled.

"All I really want right now is for the two of us stay alive. We can't wait around for God, or anyone else for that matter, to show up to save us." There was a hint of desperation in Jeff's voice as he pointed behind his back.

"And I *really* don't want the good folks from the Baptist Fellowship to take us on home to Jesus. So can we get out of here? *Now*, please?"

Megan gave him another dark look, her arms crossed as Jeff waited. He looked ready to jump up and push her out of the driver's seat. The stretch between the church and road was not that big and many of the stumbling figures had crossed most of it already, their greedy fingers stretching out to clutch at the two survivors.

"I *am* sorry Megan. I *really* am." Jeff could feel a tingling in his neck where he had been nearly strangled the day before. At the same time he was beginning to imagine an army of ghouls smashing through the window and tearing him to pieces.

Megan shook her head and grabbed a hold of the steering wheel. She stamped down on the gas pedal and the wheels spit up gravel as they caught hold of the road. Jeff was pushed back in his seat and his contrite expression changed to surprise.

"Why do you have to be such a cold hearted prick?" Megan inquired.

Jeff swallowed hard. He took a deep breath and let it blow out between his teeth before he spoke.

"I'm not trying to be. I'm just more concerned about the two human beings *inside* the minivan than I am about those things *outside* of it."

Megan didn't look happy with his answer.

"They're *dead*, Megan." Jeff could feel the anger peaking out again and stuffed it back down inside. He shrugged. "They're dead or as good as dead." Pausing, he lifted his eyes to the roof of the van and tried to search for something to say but was at a loss. He wasn't really sure what the infected actually were. Medical science hadn't offered any plausible explanations when the doctors and scientists were still alive to study the virus. But he didn't need anyone to tell him what he already knew.

"They're dead," he repeated as he looked over at her,

his eyes sad. "They just haven't figured it out yet."

He saw her grip on the steering wheel loosen. Megan was blinking fast, fighting back tears of rage. Seeing that his words were making things worse, not better, Jeff felt the bile of anger boiling up from his gut once again.

"I've mourned enough for a lifetime already. I'll be *damned* if I'm going to do it for a bunch of people I didn't even know." He crossed his arms and stared out the window.

"Maybe you *will* be damned for it."

Jeff stiffened at Megan's indictment. He looked at her and was unable to think of a response. He saw her emotions shift, from anger to regret and then sadness. She opened her mouth again to say something but snapped it shut quickly, before uttering another word. Tears began to roll freely down her face.

Jeff went back to looking out the window as he thought about what Megan had said. His desire to argue was gone and all he felt was a cold, hard lump of remorse in the pit of his stomach.

As he watched the trees roll by, he leaned his face against the window and thought about what he had become. He had no idea who he was anymore.

Maybe I am damned...maybe we all are.

Chapter 17

They rode in silence, each trapped in their own misery. Jeff tried to apologize but clammed up before barely speaking a word when Megan stiffened at the sound of his voice. So he sat, slumped shouldered, as they moved slowly down the rural road.

Large stretches of the route they took were unpopulated and a dense canopy of trees stretched to the horizon on both sides of the road. The gaps in the woodlands were filled with modest homes with large properties spread out behind them. They weren't in farm country yet but were moving further away from the densely populated suburbs.

Fifteen minutes passed before Megan finally spoke. "Maybe you should drive," she said in a stilted voice.

Jeff looked over at her, slightly confused.

"I don't know my way around Gallatin," she said, her voice losing some of its stiffness.

"Just stop whenever and we can switch," he replied in an even tone.

Megan looked over at him and nodded, her eyes filled with regret. "Thank you," she whispered.

Jeff gave her a hesitant smile. When she returned a shy one of her own he felt the tension drain away. Neither of them had found a way to say they were sorry but at least there was some kind of understanding between them. Things were going to be okay.

The van slowed to a stop and the man and woman changed places. As Jeff settled back into the driver's seat he spied something glittering in the distance. He looked out the window and squinted in the bright sunshine.

"What the hell...?"

Megan was still getting situated when she heard him speak. As she plopped into her chair she saw him peering through the windshield. Jeff's eyes widened and she squinted to try and catch a glimpse of what he was looking at. After a few moments she spotted it.

There were human shapes in the distance. Megan blinked and rubbed at her eyes. Despite her best efforts to focus the figures were not clear. All she could tell was that they were coming up over a hill perhaps a quarter of a mile down the road.

"They must have heard the engine," Megan said.

Jeff nodded absently as he continued to track the shapes moving closer. Megan noticed something else out of the corner of her eye; it was more movement. The rearview mirror was angled away from her so she moved it. There they were, behind them.

"It looks like the gangs all here."

Jeff glanced over at Megan and then turned to look out the back window. There were three, possibly four more shapes behind them and there was no doubt as to what they were. They were closer to them than the others.

He shifted the van into gear and they began rolling forward. "I'd rather deal with the ones in front of us than the ones behind." Megan nodded and quickly forgot about the shuffling ghouls to their rear.

Pressing down gently on the gas, Jeff elevated their speed to twenty as they moved closer to the people up ahead. The sunlight beating down was directly behind the little group and it was still hard to tell exactly *what* they were.

Megan gasped as she saw one waving, its arm swinging back and forth to hail them.

Jeff slowed the van down. He had seen the movement

as well. Megan squealed in excitement and clapped her hands, obviously assuming the little group before them was uninfected. He wasn't quite so sure.

As they inched closer he saw that there were three of them and they were all wearing military uniforms. Jeff's hands tightened on the steering wheel as he saw one had a rifle slung over its shoulder.

Megan turned to Jeff and punched him playfully on the arm as her smile widened. He ignored her and kept watch over the trio. Pressing gently on the brakes, he stopped the van in the middle of the road and watched the group's slow progress.

"Well, don't stop now!" Megan chastised Jeff. "We're almost to them." She giggled. "And to think, we were *this* close to a military outpost the whole time!" She was shaking her head in disbelief as she bounced in her seat in excitement.

When Jeff didn't begin moving forward again she gave an exasperated growl and leaned over to open her door. His response was instantaneous. He grabbed her by the arm and pointed at the men.

"What?" Megan shrugged out of Jeff's grasp and gave him an irritated look. He glared back in response and jabbed his finger out the windshield for emphasis.

"Would you just take another look?" he chastised her.

She ignored the request for a moment as she gave him her most withering glance. When Jeff didn't back down, Megan sighed. Rolling her eyes, she slowly looked back out the windshield, making it clear she was only doing so to get him off her back.

The soldiers had gotten much closer. Megan's jaw quivered and she felt faint.

They were definitely soldiers. More accurately, they *had* been soldiers, but now were just another group of plague victims. One was still waving at them and it looked like he was signaling their van to pull over. Jeff studied him carefully. The private had apparently been attacked with his sidearm in his hand and there it remained. Swollen fingers were sealed on the weapon, the skin cracked and dripping dark pus as his hand waved back and forth in front of him. He was dragging a mangled leg behind, forcing his arm to rise up to maintain balance. Jeff breathed a sigh of relief when he saw that the semi-automatic's slide was back. The weapon was empty.

The other two soldiers had an assortment of bruises, wounds, and ragged tears to their flesh. One was missing his lower jaw and the gaping hole down his tattered throat pulsated and bubbled. The other had an M16 hanging limply over an arm that was sliced in half. Rubbery looking gristle dangled from the wound, the remains of muscle and tissue from his absent forearm.

Megan remained silent as they began moving again and swerved around the threesome. Jeff could see the look of stunned fatigue on her face and wanted to say something to comfort her but could think of nothing. It looked like she had been beaten into submission and he immediately hated that look on her face. It filled him with despair. Even when she was angry with him it was better than this.

He picked up speed as they moved over the hill. They passed an intersection with a dead traffic light above and an over-turned Humvee off to the side. Jeff glanced at it wistfully but kept moving. There were too many places nearby for the infected to be hiding to risk getting out and checking for weapons or supplies they could use.

The road beyond the overturned military vehicle was clear for the most part and they saw houses up ahead. The van rolled slowly on and Jeff kept his eyes peeled.

The road curved to the north and he could see a clog of cars ahead and knew they were almost to Gallatin. It was not as bad as it had been in Milfield but it was clear people had been trying to escape this area as well. Most of the cars were facing the opposite direction with only a handful heading toward town.

Jeff slowed to a stop as they hit another intersection. It was a mess of cracked up cars and quite a few torn and twisted bodies; bodies that noticed the van and began moving slowly toward it. Several shapes detached themselves from their resting places in between vehicles and from the small, decimated businesses on both sides of the road.

It was a wide intersection, a major exchange. Jeff and Megan both glanced at the supermarket that took up a huge plot of land across the road. Despite the damage to the building it looked newly renovated. A shiny sign out front advertised it as a mega-mart, one of those combination grocery and everything else type of places. Any thoughts of trying to raid the massive superstore came and went as Jeff scanned the parking lot. He spied two Humvees with SAWs mounted on top, just like the one back in Milfield. Their doors were open and at least one shredded body lay nearby along with an array of military hardware that had been discarded and forgotten. They were positioned near the entrance of the store and several Jersey Barriers were set up next to them. They looked exactly like the concrete barriers used in highway construction.

There was a large group of infected milling about the parking lot looking into abandoned cars and clutching shopping carts. For the most part they had not noticed the minivan yet. Jeff looked closer and spotted even more squirming bodies behind the shattered front window of the store. There were several bright placards torn and dangling from the broken glass announcing specials on ground chuck and gallons of milk.

"It doesn't look like Gallatin did any better than Milfield," he said with a dismissive grunt as he pulled into the intersection.

There was a clear path on the road and Jeff knew the National Guard must have created it so traffic would continue to flow despite every citizen's desire to turn the thoroughfare into a giant parking lot. It was tricky navigating past the dead cars and military vehicles and he was forced to pull into the grass on the side of the road to get around several clusters of more overturned and smashed up Humvees.

Several blood soaked signs with hastily scrawled messages were tacked to several telephone poles. They all read the same: *Civilian vehicles must go north or south! Please do not abandon your vehicle on Route 28: it will be removed from the roadway. Personal items are subject to inspection and confiscation. NO civilians are allowed to carry firearms or explosives beyond this point. Violators will be shot!*

It appeared as if several makeshift checkpoints had been set up and then smashed and trampled. As Jeff and Megan looked out at the wasteland around them they fought back nausea at seeing the remains of countless dead soldiers and civilians. They were impossible to miss because they were everywhere. Thick clouds of circling flies turned the air black over the corpses.

Not only was there a wide array of severed body parts spread across the pavement and grass there was a slew of weapons as well. Jeff saw rifles, side arms, grenade launchers, and even a few flame throwers. Scorch marks on the roadway and vehicles hinted at a massive battle that must have taken place in the area. Night vision goggles, shattered and useless, were also strewn about.

Thousands of spent cartridges surrounded several heavy machine gun emplacements. They had been spit out at a tremendously high rate of speed and bounced off concrete barriers that had been set up in a feeble attempt to block the advance of what must have been a horde of the infected. They could hear the sound of countless hollow metal shells being crushed beneath the van's tires as they rolled on. All the weapons, the belt fed machine guns and the fifty-caliber M-2's, along with the grenade launchers, M16's and M4's, had fallen to the ground. Tripods and other mounting devices were smashed and broken. Jeff wondered how many useable weapons were still in the area and he felt the itch of desire to stop and snatch something up once again. The temptation passed as he saw a group of walking and tripping rotters congregating nearby. They were weaving around clusters of military equipment and he spied several shadows moving on both sides of the road, back near the buildings and behind them.

Suddenly, several ghouls popped up in front of them like jack in the boxes. It was almost as if they had magically appeared in front of the van, banging, moaning, and trying to climb on the hood as Jeff hit the brakes. Megan burst out with a high pitched squeal and Jeff shouted "Jesus Christ!" as the monsters slavered and slouched toward them.

Megan began pushing backwards in her seat, her hands pressed against the dash. "Go around. Go around. GO AROUND!" she repeated as she pulled her legs up underneath her chin, still grinding her rear against the back of her seat.

"SHUT UP AND LET ME THINK!" Jeff screamed in response.

Megan chirped one last time and then fell silent, turning her full concentration toward scrunching into the tightest ball possible. Jeff gripped the steering wheel, looking frantically out at the front of the van. For the moment the five or so stiffened figures pounding on the hood were their only immediate threat. More were coming from all directions but were further back.

He was upset with himself for having missed spotting the five stiffs before but was now totally focused on them. Two wore flak vests with the digital patterned camouflage that had become the standard with the military over the past few years. Another was in a MOPP, or chem suit, that had been ripped open, exposing a shattered rib cage. The mask had also been torn off and dangled freely from its neck. The monster's face, exposed, was free of flesh and gave Jeff a skeletal grin. The other two were civilians. None were in great shape, their clothing shredded and their flesh cracked and burnt from endless days exposed to the summer sun. But even in their present condition Jeff knew they could make some serious dents in the van if he allowed them to keep whaling on it.

There was no room to turn around. Not much possibility of driving past them either. More were coming and closing rapidly. He flipped the van in reverse and hit the gas.

Megan popped her head up from behind her knees and her eyes went wide as she felt the van moving backwards.

"Wha- what are you doing!?" The panic in her voice was rising as she repeated the question. "NO NO NO! We can't go back!" She started reaching for the wheel and Jeff swatted her hand away with a stinging slap. She pulled back and held her hand close to her chest as she gave him a horrified look, pain and terror battling for supremacy on her face.

"I'm just giving us some room to maneuver," he said as he fought to keep the wheel straight. The loud thump startled them both, but the bounce, like they had hit a large speed bump, had the minivan careening out of control. Jeff's head slammed into the headrest as they came to a stop against one of the Humvees that lined the street. He quickly recovered and looked out the back window of the Odyssey.

The rear window was splattered with a trail of something dark and viscous. It was dripping from the point of impact, where a piece of something still quivered like a blob of coagulated chocolate pudding. After a couple seconds it left a snail trail as it slid to the ground. Jeff thought he had seen a tooth in it but couldn't be sure. He flipped the car into drive and heard moaning coming from below the vehicle.

"I guess you didn't finish it off." The sudden jolt of hitting the Humvee had allowed Megan to regain some of her senses. Her arms were crossed as she chided Jeff.

He smiled and began to accelerate. "Got it covered." The next thump had a more sickly sound to it as they ran over the body again. Megan shivered involuntarily as a wet, greasy popping noise completed the effect as they rolled forward. The revulsion was short lived as she focused on the group in front of them. They were closing on the minivan.

"Brace yourself."

Megan gripped the edge of the dashboard with both hands as Jeff floored it, heading straight toward the flesh covered wall in front of them. The impact was surprisingly quiet as they plowed into the rotters. They were spread out and Jeff managed to avoid one, nick two, and only had to plow head on into the final three. One was so ripe and bloated that it exploded like a balloon, spreading its insides over the front of the vehicle.

Megan's eyes bugged out as she watched the ghastly pseudo-human disintegrate. The head must have been mush to begin with, because it did not sound or look like any bones shattered on impact. It was a piñata with eyes. But instead of candy, it was filled with a brackish jelly that ran in thick ropes down the window.

Megan attempted to bend over and put her hands down around her ankles. She felt dizzy and nauseous. Her seat belt locked, forcing her to stay upright. Acid splashed up from her stomach and caught in her throat as bits of the chips she had ate that morning regurgitated into her mouth.

Jeff nailed another stiff dead-on and its head thumped hard against the hood before it was immediately sucked under the vehicle. The last one, the one closest to him, was the tallest of the trio and the point of impact was at its midsection instead of its chest. Its legs connected with the bumper and were crushed on impact, though it seemed unconcerned as its right arm landed next to the side view mirror. It latched on to it and pulled itself onto the windshield directly in front of Jeff. Its other arm started scratching at the window.

It glared woefully at the driver. One of its eyelids was gone along with a good chunk of the bushy brow above it. The lower lip was in tatters, now just a ribbon of flesh that had gone green with some sort of bacterial growth. The ghoul pressed the ragged flap of skin onto the window's surface and formed a ring on the glass. Jeff watched, hypnotized as its shattered, yellow teeth drew little lines on the windshield as its lips opened and closed. A blackened tongue darted between them, depositing soupy globs of saliva on the glass.

Jeff's skin rose up in almost painful goose bumps as if the tongue was licking and caressing him instead of the window. He resisted the urge to flip on the windshield wipers and spray the freak with wiper fluid.

Fortunately, the ghoulish man was weak and began to slide down the hood almost immediately. Its mouth remained attached to the glass like some sort of leech, leaving a slug trail of bile behind it, until it fell and slipped under the front wheel, where the last of its life force was squished out of its mangled entrails.

Jeff hit the gas and weaved between more bodies and other obstacles as they moved down the road. Megan was still holding on to the dashboard as she stared at the floor. She was gulping down the re-circulated air that held only a taint of corruption from outside.

"That was fun," she mumbled under her breath, her head still firmly planted between her outstretched arms. To Jeff it appeared as if she was trying to push the dashboard forward. His eyes darted back to the road as he swerved to avoid another overturned Humvee.

They were coming to another intersection. The military vehicles had begun to thin out and there were none up ahead. The road was actually clear for a small stretch. There were two gas stations situated across from one another, both with fast food joints connected to them. One was a McDonalds and the other was a popular local chili joint. Megan's stomach growled and she gagged. Her hand slammed over her mouth as she fought the urge to vomit once again.

Jeff reached out and then retracted his hand before he could rub her back in comfort. He wasn't sure how Megan would react as he watched her fight to keep the small amount of food she had eaten down. He relaxed slightly as she seemed to gain control, though she was still breathing hard and staring at the floor.

Jeff looked back outside and studied the area they were moving into. Paying little attention to the buildings, he instead focused on the strands of concertina wire that ran from the front edge of one of the gas stations to the other across the road. A few jersey barriers ran the gap and wire was pinned to each, running for several feet between each concrete road block. It ran the entire width of the road and into the parking lots. Some of the wire had fallen, either cut or smashed. The gaps created were big enough to drive a car through. In other places it still held, and several of the infected had cut themselves to ribbons trying to get through it. Various spots ran red with blood and chunks of flesh hung like streamers from the razor wire. As the minivan got closer, the engine seemed to agitate the ghouls near the wall and they began to move as one toward them. Several shambled through the open gaps while others got tangled in the wire. They fought against it, ignoring their predicament as they continued to get more tangled. Jeff had to look away as the razor wire began to cut deeply into their flesh. The rest of his view was equally unpleasant as he saw more dead bodies scattered throughout the area. Some were sprawled on the ground while others dangled over the concrete barriers.

"Which way are we going?" Megan mumbled in a faint voice.

Jeff pressed harder on the gas. Steering the wheel to the right, he turned onto Gallatin Road. It was essentially Main Street for the town.

"The local schools are down this way. That's probably where any emergency shelters were set up," he said as he looked over at his passenger. Some normal color had returned to her face and she no longer looked like she was going to barf on the floorboards. "I figured we should check them out."

Megan nodded and looked out the window. The houses on both sides of the street showed signs of severe damage. That captured her attention more than the abundance of infected roaming the area. She furrowed her brow and looked from house to house. Back in Milfield the damage had been random, chaotic. Not so in Gallatin. Every home here was in bad shape.

There were clots of stiff legged figures spilling out the doors and windows to take random swipes at them. Jeff almost laughed as one of the figures toppled over on a driveway from its efforts to grab them even though it was nowhere near close enough.

Megan looked away from the houses and their occupants and stared at the street. There was plenty of shattered glass and blood splashed on...everything. Bones were tossed and piled everywhere and the cars that lined the road looked as bad as the houses.

"I think...I think maybe this isn't such a good idea."

Jeff didn't hear Megan's hesitant words as he focused on the road and kept them moving at a slow and steady pace. Megan twisted around in her seat to better see the infected following them. There was no consistency to their movement, no locked step efficiency. Still, there was symmetry to it. All eyes were locked on the van like it was a homing beacon. Their arms were elevated as they reached out toward their prize. She was amazed at how quickly they fell into a line behind the van. More came from the sides of the road as the vehicle passed, crawling over one another, desperate to get close. As they continued to roll down the road the crowd behind grew larger.

Jeff pressed the gas a bit harder and the crowd fell back. They rolled over a small hill and the squalid mass dipped out of sight, though there were still more joining it as the van drove on.

The road ahead was fairly clear, as far as they could see. It was straight but the gradual slope made it impossible to see more than a few hundred feet ahead. Jeff guessed that if it were true that the Gallatin high school and middle schools were set up as emergency shelters that in all likelihood the National Guard had kept the road clear of civilian vehicles. The machine gun positions in the front yards of several houses and detour signs on the side streets they passed seemed to confirm his theory.

"Almost there."

When Jeff looked over at Megan he saw terror etched on her face. His grin of confidence went slack and he began to slow down.

"Megan? What is it?"

She did not respond immediately. Instead, she kept looking ahead, toward the schools. A water tower stood nearby, its rusted struts climbing skyward, the fat metal belly painted with wording letting them know they were in Clermont County. Beyond it she could see the outlines of several large brick buildings on both sides of the road.

A church was to the left, partially blocking the view of another, larger building behind it. The only real indication that it was a house of worship and not a rather large home, at least from the angle Megan was looking from, was the steeple that shot like an arrow straight to heaven. Several ground floor windows were boarded up but otherwise it looked to be in good shape. Several of the windows were shattered but the boards were still in place behind them.

Past the church were several squat buildings that were obviously schools. Plain and drab with large windows that peered into classrooms, they fit the mold of most modern educational facilities. Squared off and bland, there were two elementary schools and a junior high sharing the same parking lot.

On the other side of the road past the chain link fence surrounding the water tower was the high school. It was larger than the other schools and looked more modern. A small parking lot was wedged between the tower and the school and a much bigger one ran around the back of the building all the way to the far side. The high school was closer to them than the church but stretched far down the road so that it was also across from the elementary schools.

Megan was surprised to see how far down the road the entire campus went. She could not see anywhere near the edge of the property lines of the schools-they were simply too far away. On both the road and the wide expanse of grass in front of the high school were more abandoned military vehicles and gun emplacements. There was plenty of room to maneuver and allow the van to glide by the remnants of what equipment had been abandoned there.

It was quiet. Megan squinted as she looked around. There were no bodies slumped over like up the street and none up and walking around. She could see no movement in the shadows.

They would be past the water tower soon.

The serenity of the scene did nothing to change the look of raw fear on Megan's face.

"Jeff, just keep driving. I don't want to stop here. I don't think it's a good idea." Her words were steady and concise but Jeff could hear the panic beneath them. When she grabbed his arm and he looked at her he knew she was struggling to remain calm.

He stared into her eyes and was amazed at how deeply blue they were. He knew it was a strange time to notice but they stood out prominently against the dark circles underneath them and Megan's olive skin tone. They were luminescent, shining like beacons in an otherwise hollowed out and ravaged visage.

Her look of desperation passed and so did Jeff's feeble attempt at a smile. Suddenly he felt incredibly uncomfortable as those blazing blue eyes locked onto his and her fingers began digging into his skin.

Jeff swung his head around and looked at the scene in front of them. Everything seemed quiet. The buildings looked normal, though the heavy artillery in the street was out of place.

There was a sign on the right side of the road with a bright red arrow on it. It was pointing at the high school. There was some sort of text on it below the arrow but Jeff could not make it out. After his quick survey of the area he turned back to Megan.

"I don't see what's got you all worked up. I mean..." he waved his hand in front of him, "look around us. There's no one here. At least none of those things."

"JEFF! We *can't* stop here. Please, just keep driving. I think we'll be in big trouble if we stop. I don't know why, it's just..." Megan's voice got louder as she kept speaking and there was almost a hysterical edge to it.

"Now hold on!" Jeff shook off her death grip on his arm. "Just chill out!"

"No. No. NO. NO!" Each negation was punctuated by a violent shake of her head.

Suddenly, they were yelling at each other. Megan's voice reached a frenzied pitch as Jeff allowed the van coast forward. When he did, she tried sliding her foot onto the gas but he blocked it and applied gentle pressure to the brake.

As she continued to bark and plead in his ear, Jeff looked out at the sign in front of the high school, which he could read now. He just wanted to read it and kept repeating that desire to Megan but she was ignoring everything he said.

Megan suddenly stopped screaming and took a deep breath as she tried to compose herself. "Jeff, listen to me. *Please.*" Her volume had decreased dramatically. Jeff was still seething, still angry at her seemingly out of left field outburst but waited to hear what she had to say as he stared at the sign.

GALLATIN EMERGENCY SHELTER. ALL FAMILIES AND INDIVIDUALS REPORT TO THE GYM FOR REGISTRATION.

One suitcase per family, clothes only. No pets! All food and water will be provided. All food and water brought on the premises will be confiscated. NO FIREARMS! Please have valid state or federal ID available for inspection. Thank you for your cooperation.

A large arrow ran the length of the sign and pointed toward an entrance to the high school they couldn't see from their position. The faculty parking lot was visible to their right, crammed with an assortment of cars. A few had slammed into the rest and their doors were wide open. They had been abandoned in a hurry. The student parking lot was on the far side of the building, where the main doors probably were. The much larger lot was even more clogged than the faculty lot. A few Humvees were mixed in with the cars, strategically placed at the entrances to funnel traffic.

"There's nobody here, Jeff. No one." Megan began. "No one normal, at least. I think we should just go." Her words were calm but intense. "I think we should head down the road and not look back. Please Jeff, just leave now, God, I know this is gonna get bad, I just know it...please..."

She was becoming hysterical again but Jeff was not paying attention as she continued to ramble. Instead, he was squinting toward the glass doors of the high school. His eyes tried to focus at the shadowy darkness beyond them. He swore he could see movement.

"I think..." Jeff said, his voice distant.

Megan suddenly stopped speaking. "What?" she asked, her eyes glued to him. She had not heard his quiet words.

He didn't respond immediately as he shook his head in anger. "Son of a bitch," he mumbled under his breath.

"I think you're right," he sighed and nodded toward the doors of the school.

As Megan swiveled her head she saw the doors to the high school had already been pushed open by a mass of infected bodies spilling out onto the lawn. She watched in stunned silence as more and more of them tumble through the doors in a mad rush to get to the van.

"Fuck!"

Megan jumped as Jeff cursed. He was looking at the other side of the street. More ghouls were pouring out of each of the other school buildings. They were a flood, smashing through the doors and windows as they came.

Jeff slammed his foot on the gas and the van shot

forward. As they flew by the ongoing mess, he laughed nervously "Jesus H. Christ! How many people lived in Gallatin!? Fuck me!" He spoke with a nervous enthusiasm and a hint of stunned awe. "There are *way* too many people here."

His eyes never left the growing crowds that were about to merge on the street behind them. He gunned the engine to sixty. It amazed him that bodies were still pouring out the schools.

"Jeff...JEFF! Look out!" Megan screamed in his ear. He swung his head back around and swallowed hard as he slammed on the brakes.

The military had not only built a wall back up the road, they had built one here as well, at the edge of the school campus. Neither Jeff nor Megan had seen it when they had stopped and were too busy gawking at the crowds behind them to notice until they were almost on top of it. This wall was different than the other one. There were no concrete barriers or razor wire this time, just a row of trucks stretching across the road and into the grass on both sides.

The anti-lock brakes on the van kicked in and they grinded to a halt short of the wall. Jeff quickly turned the vehicle around to face the oncoming horde.

Megan looked behind them at the assortment of big rigs and military troop transports that had been cobbled together to form the barricade. As she looked closer she saw wire peeking out from the various openings and nooks that might allow someone to sneak through. She quickly realized that much of it had already been pushed out of the way and there was movement on the other side of the vehicles. As she looked closer, several hands peaked through, grabbing for purchase as they pulled and scratched their way over and under the mechanical fortification.

"We're gonna have company behind us pretty quick."

Jeff ignored the comment as he focused on what was in front of them: the schools, the jammed parking lots, and wooded areas beyond. The van was no 4x4 and would not make it off road. Heading back the way they had come was becoming less of an option every second. A line of infected were strung from one side of the road to the other, three deep at the weakest points and thicker in most places. There were a few gaps, but nothing they could plow through.

There were hundreds of them and more were coming. They were creeping over and around the trucks behind them and the buildings ahead kept dispensing an endless supply of corpselike bodies. The infected were everywhere.

Gritting his teeth, Jeff turned to Megan. She was afraid but looked composed, surprisingly enough. Her semi-calm state helped him stay cool as he spoke.

"I think we have one chance. It's not a good one, but …"

Megan nodded, ready for him to get on with it. She looked at the slowly advancing army and reached for her revolver. Gripping it tightly, she stared ahead.

Looking out into the crowd of rabid faces, Megan locked onto one. It stood out as different in the sea of grey, green, and black rot that covered most of them. It had been an adult, probably a man, although most of its scalp had been torn or ripped away and gave no hint as to its hairstyle. Its clothing, a shredded tee shirt and what were probably blue jeans that had been split up the seams, also gave no clues. There were no breasts but the stomach was swollen, filled with corrupt fluid and undigested meat. What stood out about this one, what had made her zero in on it, was the face. It was purple. It was not bloated and the damage was minimal. Both eyes remained; set deep within a sea of violet flesh that drooped but still retained the shape of a human visage. They were pig eyes. The purple wasn't just old dead veins showing through the skin filled with drying blood, it was as if the ghoul had been dipped in dye. Megan hadn't seen a stiff quite that hue before. She gripped the gun tighter as she realized that it was staring back at her.

Jeff floored the minivan and turned the wheel sharply to the right, heading for the wide parking lot that the junior high and elementary schools shared. Between the two buildings was a massive glut of ghouls and behind them a small road running between the buildings. He swiftly dismissed the idea of trying to get past the crowd and down the road when he saw a logjam of more vehicles there that would prevent their escape.

"Hang on; this might get a little rough."

Megan braced herself as the van dipped down and quickly rose back up as they traversed the shallow ditch at the edge of the parking lot. She shifted the revolver to her left hand and gripped the handle above her door. They avoided the paved entrance to the lot, which was crowded with bodies. The van went airborne for a split second and landed roughly on the pavement.

Megan closed her eyes and cringed as several bodies bounced off the bumper. As the fat rear end of the Odyssey swung sideways she heard more bodies being knocked over behind them. Jeff floored it again, spinning the wheel frantically left and right, trying to avoid the larger pockets of rotters. He moved in close to the junior high and at the last moment turned sharply to the left, weaving around like he was on an obstacle course. More and more thuds were heard as the infected bounced off the van in rapid succession.

Jeff gripped the wheel like he was strangling it, refusing to let it direct him, which it seemed desperate to do as the front wheels continued to hit more and more bodies and were forced to turn in directions different than he wanted to go. His foot hit the gas and brake in rapid succession as he slalomed around the human pylons he was trying to avoid.

They worked their way across the parking lot toward the church and Jeff set his sights on the road. They had to try and return the way they had come. It was the only reasonably clear path remaining. The crowd heaved and quivered like a single entity and refused to grant the leeway they needed.

Jeff hit the brakes. A moving fortification of bodies

was closing in from the front and sides. He looked in the rearview mirror, hoping he could throw the minivan in reverse. Seeing it was even worse behind them, he knew going forward was their only option. The bodies were several deep up front but the driver knew if he could gun the engine and build up some speed the van might be able to break through.

That's when he saw the others: the crowd that had been following the van from the intersection, the ones they had left behind not so long ago. The newcomers were getting closer and blending in with the infected from the schools creating an impenetrable wall of rotten meat in front of them.

A whimper escaped Jeff's throat. He had forgotten all about them. The horrid parade of infected streamed down the road, swelling the ranks of the hoard. In no time they would overwhelm the van and crush it with their sheer volume. There was no place left to go.

"I'm so sorry."

Jeff couldn't look at Megan as he spoke. A cacophony of moans surrounded them, rising in pitch and increasing in volume by the millisecond. The ghouls would be on top of the van in moments.

"I am so sorry Megan...so, so, sorry."

He felt her finger sliding under his chin, raising it up. Jeff tried to avert his eyes, but Megan moved his face toward hers. He felt her lips, cool and dry, on his cheek.

He opened his red tinged eyes. They were bloodshot, tired, and sunken. He had nothing left to offer, but Megan was smiling at him. She looked calm, almost serene.

Touching his face with her hands she retained her grip on the gun. She shook her head to quiet Jeff. "This isn't your fault. None of it is." She touched his forehead with hers and they huddled together, the gun cold and rigid against Jeff's cheek, contradicting the warm and human touch of Megan's hands. They looked at one another and realized that there was nothing left to say. All that mattered was that they were together.

The pounding on the van began and the vehicle started slowly moving under the blows. The moans were overwhelming. The two survivors embraced one last time, Jeff nodding when Megan slipped the gun down between them. She held it and waited.

More ghouls swarmed the minivan, climbing over one another in a desperate attempt to reach the warm, living flesh that called to them.

Chapter 18

Jeff could hear the pistol cock, but only because it was so close to his ear. They had wrapped their arms around each other as the fists began to reign down. The minivan shook gently at first, as the moans intermingled with the wet slapping of rotten flesh against glass and metal. The vehicle held up to the muffled thuds initially, the infected unable to force their way inside as they rammed their bodies against every square inch of exterior space. But as more crowded and pressed against one another they were starting to have an impact.

The moans erupting from two thousand corrupted throats began to overwhelm the constant and thunderous hammering of fists. It rose in pitch and seemed to unify into an unholy sound as if it came from a single creature howling in rage.

As Jeff waited, he became puzzled. The final moment he had been dreading was not happening. The glass was not shattering and the doors were not being ripped open. Listening carefully, after a few seconds he thought he could detect a decrease in the amount of fists pounding on the exterior of the van. Fighting a nearly paralyzing fear, he opened his eyes.

Loosening his clinch around Megan, Jeff gently pushed her back toward her seat. Bewildered, she opened her eyes and timidly mumbled "what?" in a childlike voice.

Jeff stared out the window, baffled by what he saw. Many of the creatures remained nearby, smashing their bodies against the quarter panels, but those at the edge of the crowd were drifting away. Jeff, then Megan, watched as more of the mob peeled off, especially out front. The sounds emanating from outside were jagged, not in harmony as they had been moments before. Confusion rippled through the crowd.

Jeff sat rigidly in his seat trying to puzzle out what was happening. A path was clearing in front of the van, gradually. Not enough to allow him to drive away, but more and more of the foul creatures were wandering off.

"What are they doing?"

"I have no idea."

He searched the crowd. It was hard to see much of anything that would give him an idea what was going on. He puzzled over the possibilities. What could be more important to the cannibalistic and homicidal infected than a couple of fresh bodies, probably the only two within miles?

His mind raced with possibilities. Leaning forward, Jeff squinted as he tried to peer through the gaps forming in the crowd. Following the path of stiffs that had turned away from the minivan, he could see they were all moving in the same direction. It was a straight line going past the high school. He strained his eyes and cursed silently. Still looking, his eyes darted back and forth, trying to find a better angle. Then he stopped, frozen, and saw what was drawing the infected's attention.

"Oh my God..."

"What? What is it?" Megan looked at Jeff and tried to follow his line of sight, but it was hard for her to pick out anything even as he pointed at the water tower. There was a sudden intake of breath as Megan finally spied what he was looking at.

At the water tower was the source of the crowd's interest: a man had climbed the fence and was sitting on top of it, his feet dangling on both sides. He was waving his arms and whooping at the ghouls, luring them away from the van.

"There. Holy Jesus, what the hell is he doing?" Jeff said, his voice coming out in a confused croak.

The man hanging on top of the fence was yelling like a maniac at the plague victims moving slowly toward him.

"He's trying to save us." There was wonder in Megan's voice. She looked over at Jeff, her eyes alight with hope, and saw the stunned expression on his face.

"Jeff? JEFF!" Megan began to shout at him repeatedly as he continued to stare at the madman on the fence.

Finally, he blinked and looked at her.

"What're we going to do?" She pleaded.

Jeff looked back at the man who was currently swinging a leg over the chain link fence so he could drop inside the enclosure. Once inside he would be trapped. There was no ladder leading up to the top of the water tower. The fence looked rusty and probably wouldn't hold up under much pressure. The infected were too clumsy to climb, but it would still collapse under their weight within minutes.

The man dropped down inside the small corral as the first of the creatures got close enough to grab for him. He was lost from their sight as more of the rotters crowded the fence, blocking the view.

"Jeff?" Megan didn't shout this time, but she was demanding an answer.

Before he could say anything something came crashing down in front of them and clobbered two of the pus bags near the van. They were knocked sprawling, one tumbling into the other as something compact slammed into its skull.

Jeff immediately tried to figure out where the missile had come from. As he did, something else slammed into the back of a one armed man dressed in a tattered business suit. He followed the object as it went spinning down to the pavement in the church parking lot. It was a book.

A wide circle of infected surrounding the area where the book had landed turned as one and stared up at the second floor of the church.

Megan noticed the attack as well and watched in silence as more books flew from one of the windows of the church and crashed into the group that had suddenly lost all interest in the van as well as the man at the water tower.

As they both peered at the window, an arm popped out. Another man, waving and screaming in the same suicidal fashion as the one at the tower, was climbing out onto the roof of the church. He was African American and as Jeff looked closer, he realized he was just a kid. He was too thin and gangly to be an adult.

The crowd had splintered entirely, with a large portion starting to assault the church.

"How many of these people are there?" Megan asked. Her voice was still awestruck but laced with excitement.

"I have no idea, but they're fucking nuts." Jeff couldn't keep the admiration out of his voice.

"We have to help them," Megan said, distracted, as she watched the kid on the roof send more of the books piled in his arms sailing into the crowd. He flipped the ghouls off and laughed as he sent another tome smashing into a police officer's chest.

Megan turned to Jeff and tugged at his shirt sleeve.

She waited until he could tear his eyes away from the boy on the roof before speaking. "I don't have any clue *who* they are or *why* they chose to risk their lives for us but we can't leave them here to die." She shook her head for emphasis. "We just can't!"

"I know, I know." Jeff nodded and smiled gravely. As he gave another quick glance out the windshield at the situation unfolding in front of them his expression began to change. Megan could see the determined look on his face. There were still a few fiends bashing away at the van but that was just background noise. Most had wandered off to deal with the man at the water tower or the boy taunting them.

"I have an idea."

Chapter 19

The van was doing about forty when it plowed through the fence and smashed into five ghouls attached to it. The man standing behind the chain link dove out of the way as it collapsed and wrapped around the front of the van. The infected were pinned to the grill, prisoners of the rusty metal pressing against their bodies. The bar running along the top of the fence popped up and collapsed on the Odyssey. As the van skidded to a halt under the water tower the five hitchhikers on the hood collapsed to the ground in a tangle, stunned.

The newly discovered survivor was already getting back to his feet when Jeff rolled down his window.

"Get in!"

The cargo door began to gradually open. Megan stood ready behind it with the .357 in hand and saw that the man looked a little dazed and scratched up from his dive to the pavement but otherwise fine.

He began moving toward the open door. Megan's eyes darted back and forth. The crowd of infected seemed slightly off their game from the fierce assault, but were already starting to discover the giant, gaping hole in the fence. She waved her hand furiously to the man as he stumbled and then dove headlong through the doorway, collapsing to the floor.

"Go! Go! Go!" She yelled as the door began to shut. There were several heavy thuds as Jeff flipped the van in reverse and hit the gas. Their new passenger desperately grabbed a hold of the back of a seat and slid his hand up to the arm rest, wrapping his fingers around it tightly as they continued to fly backwards onto the street.

They skidded to a halt in the middle of the road. Jeff gave a quick look back at the man who had risked his life for him and Megan. He had gotten to his knees and was trying to slide into one of the chairs. Tall and muscular, he looked middle aged. His blond hair was going grey at the temples and there were careworn lines on his face.

"Sorry about that. I didn't know how else to get to you."

The newcomer looked up at Jeff as he plopped into the chair and then looked over at Megan, who tried to give him a reassuring smile. He tried to return it but looked out of breath.

"How many of you are over at that church? Is there anyone besides the kid on the roof?" The blond haired man raised his hand to hold off more questions until he was able to take a deep breath.

"Just the boy," he replied in a breathless huff. The words were shaky but spoken in a rich baritone.

"Okay." Jeff nodded and turned back toward the wheel. "I hope he sees us coming." The new passenger reached forward and gripped the handle on the back of Jeff's chair tightly.

The van took off like a shot. After doing a one-eighty, with bodies that got in the way flying in every direction, they sped toward the church parking lot.

Jeff avoided a large group of infected but bumped several more singles as they sped across the road. The windshield had several hairline cracks in it but had survived the assault on the fence. Pulling into the driveway, he glanced up toward the group of windows he had seen the books being flung out of. The kid was still there, waving frantically at them.

"I hope he figures out what we're doing," Jeff said

through gritted teeth.

He drove close to the building, turning the wheel and maneuvering so they were right next to the wall, just below the windows. The roof was flat so the boy could safely run right over to the van. Jeff adjusted the vehicle until it was flush with the wall. His own door was too close to the building to open so he jumped from his seat and grabbed his gore stained bat.

His two passengers watched as Jeff moved to the side door and glanced out the window. He reached for the handle.

"Excuse me," he said and the other man, stunned, got out of his way. The door slid open and Jeff gripped the bloody weapon in both hands. "Shut the door behind me please."

Megan watched Jeff jumped out as several infected closed on him. She could not swear to it but thought she heard him say "batter up!" as his feet touched the ground. As stunned as the man they had just saved looked, he reached for the handle to shut the heavy automatic door as requested.

Megan glanced over at him. He cut an impressive figure. Even sitting she could tell he would stand a couple of inches over six feet and was lean and muscular. The slightly graying hair and creases in the skin near his eyes made her guess he was probably in his late forties. He looked fit and athletic, which stood out as a stark contrast to her emaciated frame.

The confusion on his face looked comical to her. Megan gave him a sympathetic smile.

"Don't worry," she said. "He does this all the time."

They both turned to watch as the wild-haired crazy man outside the van took aim and sent an infected soldier sailing off to the side; a spray of pus erupting from where the bat made contact with his head.

Jeff yelled, whooping it up as he got into a groove. He twisted around and sent another dark shape stumbling back as he drove the top of the bat through its jaw. He could feel the adrenaline kicking in after being paralyzed with fear just minutes before.

He yelled, "Hey kid! Jump down. Come on, move it!" Jeff didn't look back as his bat connected with another soldier's arm, shattering its humerus. He kicked at the chest of a store clerk hissing and drooling at him, sending it toppling to the pavement.

"Move it kid! Haul ass!"

Ramming the aluminum bat into the mouth of another rotter, Jeff forced it backwards into the next one coming for him. They tumbled over like bowling pins as he backed up toward the van. They were running out of time.

The thud startled him but when he glanced back he felt relief. There was a grunt, and the sound of sneakers hitting asphalt as the young boy landed by the van door, anxiously waiting to get inside.

"Glad you could make it."

Jeff smiled at the gangly African American kid. He was thin, lanky, and tall for his age. The kid didn't return the smile but turned toward the van as the door opened. The older man grabbed him, yanking him inside. Jeff surveyed the area: another body closing in but still a few feet away. He backed up quickly, dismissing the idea of getting in one last hit and followed the boy. As soon as he got in Megan, who had moved to the driver's seat, pressed a button next to the steering wheel and the automatic door began to shut.

"Let's go!"

Even before the words had left Jeff's mouth Megan had them speeding away as a thick knot of fiends closed in. They moved in reverse as she steered them away from the church until they were facing the street. She flipped gears and floored it.

"Yeahhhh!" Jeff yelled as he moved to the passenger seat up front. "I can't believe we made it!" He took several breaths as Megan and the other man began to laugh. At first it was nervous but then the floodgates opened and they were all clapping and cheering as they flew down the road. Even the stoic looking boy cracked a grin.

There were handshakes and hugs all around as introductions were made. Megan was patted on the back as she headed up the road and beamed smiles at Jeff and their brand new friends.

The man's name was George. The boy was Jason. They had been stuck in the Gallatin United Methodist Church since fleeing the high school across the street several weeks back, when a huge mob of the infected swept through and wiped out the National Guard contingent assigned to protect the refugees. They had been hiding out ever since, living on a diet of juice boxes, crackers, and candy bars that had been stored for the preschool taught at the church.

"You're the first people we've seen since..." George's eyes got moist as he looked back at the mob slowly following them. He couldn't continue and no one spoke. Jeff and Megan could only imagine the nightmare George and Jason had faced when the shelter had fallen and everyone they knew had succumbed to the virus.

After a couple of minutes they returned to the intersection with the concertina wire and jersey barriers stretched across the road. Megan brought the van to an idle and everyone tried smiling nervously at one another, still unsure of what they should be talking about now that they had escaped the horde.

They looked out over the intersection. Most of the infected were behind them and it looked clear except for a few stragglers. They were struggling to move their shattered bodies close to the van but posed no immediate threat.

Megan turned to face the others. "Well?" When they were all looking at her she continued. "We're free of that mess, thanks to George and Jason," she nodded at them and Jeff leaned back to give them both a hearty slap on the back. Everyone smiled again.

"So where to now?"

The smiles quickly faded as they all looked back outside. The euphoria of their victory was already dissipating as George and Jason started realizing what had become of the world while they had hidden in the darkened church over the past month.

After a few seconds with no suggestions from the newcomers, Jeff piped up. "I'm not sure about you guys, but I vote we stick to the plan Megan and I had. We head out to the country and see if we can find someplace to hole up in and fortify." When his suggestion didn't meet with immediate nods of agreement, he added, "There'll probably be a lot less of those things out there."

Jason turned away, his expression icy as he stared out at the road. Jeff wasn't sure why the boy seemed upset, but knew there was always a reason for a kid his age to be moody. That was true even when the world was doing just fine. With the way it was now, Jason had plenty to be pissed about.

"I need to get to my family. They're up north, near Wildwood."

Everyone was suddenly looking at George. Even Jason cocked his head to the side, a confused look on his face. Apparently what George had said was as much a news blast to him as it was to Jeff and Megan.

"They're hiding out in our house," George explained. "They barricaded themselves inside when everything started going to hell in a hand basket. I was stuck in Gallatin on business and got dragged out of my hotel room and then thrown into that damn high school gymnasium." His eyes glinted with desperation. "I *have* to get to them."

When sympathetic looks began to appear on everyone's faces George started looking frustrated.

"Look, I spoke to my wife and made *sure* she understood what to do. I told her how to barricade the house. She knew what was going on. I-"

"When was the last time you spoke to her?"

Jeff felt embarrassed for interrupting. His voice was gentle when he asked the question, but he could see the irritation it caused George.

"I know what you're thinking. You know as well as I do I couldn't have spoken to her in the last month. Cell phones crapped out weeks ago. All I know is that the last time we *did* talk she was prepared to sit tight and wait for me, no matter how long it took." His eyes moved back and forth from Jeff to Megan as his frustration grew. "She can take care of herself. You don't know her! I KNOW they're okay. I *need* to get back to them!"

"Look, George, we've all lost family. It's hard to accept, I know..." Megan's voice was filled with empathy as she reached out to touch his hand.

"LISTEN to me God Dammit! I am not screwing around or suffering from delusions! MY WIFE AND KIDS ARE AT HOME AND I HAVE TO GET TO THEM, RIGHT NOW!"

Jeff felt his stomach clench as George began to shake with rage. His meaty hands were balled into fists and the strong, athletic man looked like he was ready to tear someone's head off.

Megan still had the van in drive and suddenly slammed the gearshift into park. She practically flew out of her seat at George, her jaw tight and her eyes glowing with fury. She was a tiny blur as she slid between the two captain's chairs and was inches from his face before he could even react. All Jeff and Jason could do was watch as her index finger, like a dagger, stabbed at the big man.

"No, George. YOU listen to ME!"

She was practically on top of him, looming over the man that was literally twice her size.

"I watched my husband *die* right in front of me." Every word was punctuated by her tiny finger poking George in the chest. She waved her arm around. "We've *all* lost people we love!" Rolling her eyes, she laughed bitterly. "Hell, we've all lost EVERYTHING!"

Jeff watched in amazement as George seemed at a loss as to how to deal with this tiny whirlwind that had slammed on top of him like a ton of bricks. He was still angry, but

Megan's words seemed to be having an effect on him.

"We're *all* dealing with this shit, okay? I don't know if your family is alive or dead but I *do* know one thing." She paused for effect. "I'm still alive and so are you. All four of us are *still* alive!"

Megan's anger suddenly disappeared and her entire demeanor changed. George looked stunned, as if someone had landed a solid right-cross to his jaw. Megan slowly moved her hand toward his face. Her eyes had softened and seemed to be holding the big man hypnotized. He was too astonished to resist as her fingers gently touched his cheek. She moved her other hand up to his face as well.

A single tear tried to force its way out between his lids but George blinked it away. He shifted uncomfortably as Megan spoke again.

"George." It was a whisper. The gentleness of it gave him pause. "You don't know how much I hope your family is alive. How much I hope *anyone* is alive. We want to help you George, but we need to help ourselves first. Please understand."

He stared back at Megan, his face rigid as if carved from stone. Suddenly, it began to crumble. When he reached up to grab her tiny hands with his own, tears began to roll down his face. She stood in front of him, dwarfed by his bulk as she slid her spindly arms around his neck. She leaned in close and George's hands wrapped around her. He hugged her tightly, racked with sobs that had no sound but shook his entire body.

Jeff watched until he was sure things were under control and then slid into the driver's seat. He snapped on his seatbelt and flipped the gearshift back into Drive.

When he felt like things had settled down enough, he decided to speak. "Okay guys. For now, let's just head east. We can talk about where we want to go after we get the heck away from this hellhole." No one responded as he turned the van onto the road and through one of the gaps in the razor wire that had failed to keep the infected at bay.

They were heading out into the country. Several of the ghouls that had gotten close while the van was stationary howled and swiped at it as it drove away, angry and sad at being cheated.

Chapter 20

As the quartet drove east, they saw fewer buildings, less houses, and more wide stretches of farmland. There was plenty of damage off in the distance-it looked like the area had been hit by a tidal wave. They only saw a few shadowy figures skulking around but weren't fooled. Plenty of ghouls were still out there, hiding behind barns and in the shadows, waiting for the survivors to stop and step out of the minivan.

After a while they were able to settle back and pretend everything was normal as the scenery rolled by. There were split rail fences that ran great distances and while there were few businesses, several large propane tank parks broke up the monotony of the farmland.

They passed a sign indicating the speed limit was now fifty-five. Jeff smiled when he saw it. There was the occasional abandoned vehicle in the road but not much else to worry about. He could do a hundred and it probably wouldn't cause any issues. Still, he kept the van at around thirty miles an hour. He was in no hurry to get to the next town and its heavy population just yet.

"Hey! Look, over there!"

Megan and George whipped around, startled at Jason's sudden outburst. He was pointing at one of the fields on the side of the road. Jeff shifted in his seat and slowed the van slightly so he could see what had the kid so excited.

There was another split rail fence running alongside

the road, unbroken, for at least a mile. A large building set back at least a hundred feet served as the backdrop. It was nearly as long as the fence, a huge barn made of sheet metal. It was too far away for anyone to tell if it had been attacked. Not that the building was drawing their attention. They were more interested in the horse grazing in the pasture in front of the barn.

The swayback was brown and gently nuzzling the overgrown grass. It did not bother raising its head as they slowly passed. Instead, it continued to munch contentedly. There was nothing special about the beast. It was like any other horse they had seen before. Old and grizzled, it's back dipped precariously toward the ground. All in all, it was nothing special.

Except that it was still alive.

They watched the animal with a sad intensity that would have seemed odd just a few weeks back. But that was before the plague had come. The four survivors could only guess at what the virus did to animals it came in contact with. They had no idea if it simply killed them or caused the same sort of psychosis evident in infected human beings. Only one thing was certain: someone who turned into one of those monsters would attack any living creature it could get its hands on. Most domesticated animals hadn't stood a chance against them.

Jeff turned back around as his three passengers continued to stare at the horse until it was out of sight. Jason smiled briefly, proud of his discovery, but his stoic countenance returned as they went over a rise and the field faded from view.

A few minutes later Jeff glanced at a sign telling him they were leaving Clermont County. They were out of the metropolitan area now, although there were still plenty of smaller population centers to contend with down the road. But Jeff knew if they could avoid back tracking or heading north, where George's family and a thousand of others just like his were, they might live to see another day.

Jeff was still thinking about where they should go when something caught his eye.

"There ya go!"

"What?"

Megan had been relaxing when she responded to Jeff's excited statement. She jumped up and looked out the window, fearful of what she might see. After no boiling mass of stiff bodies appeared in front of the van, she let her heart rate slow a bit. Scanning the horizon, she saw no obvious dangers and pursed her lips, trying to figure out what had gotten Jeff so worked up.

There was a large field off to their left. It ran parallel to their route for about three quarters of a mile and stretched about the same distance back from the road. A dirt path led to two squat structures in the middle of the barren field that appeared as little more than tiny dots from where they sat.

Jeff stopped the minivan. "That's the ticket, lady and gents." He turned to face the others. "We can park our butts there for the night."

George slid over and shared a window view with Jason. "It certainly looks abandoned." He was already scanning the area for anything that might give them trouble. The flat field stretched away from the homestead on the three sides they could see and it looked like the tree line behind the buildings was far back from it as well. They should be able to detect anything that tried to get close long before it became a viable threat.

"Guys, I don't know..." Megan hesitated.

"Megan, we have to find a place to stay." Jeff began. "I'm not all that interested in staying in the van tonight. I'd rather find a comfortable bed, or even a dirt floor, and just spread out and relax for a while. I'm sure George and Jason would agree-"

"You've got my vote," Jason piped up.

Jeff nodded and then looked at George. The blond man shrugged, seemingly indifferent to the idea. Jeff turned back to Megan.

"I'm all for it too, but I just think there might be a better place to try and stay than this." Megan waved her hand at the shacks dismissively. "They don't look like much."

"Well it's not the Hilton, that's for sure." Jeff agreed. "But if we set up a watch we can make sure none of those bastards sneak up on us. We can probably see for a couple of miles in all directions from those windows. That'll give us plenty of time to take off if things go wrong."

George slowly nodded in agreement as he listened to Jeff's argument. A resigned look appeared on Megan's face.

"Okay, but just for one night."

"Then it's settled." Jeff said as he grinned at her.

There were a few moments of silence as they all looked across the field together; sizing up what they hoped would be their new residence for the rest of the day and on through the night. There was still no movement any of them could see.

"Okay. Let's do this." Jeff flipped the van in reverse and backed it up to the crossroad. A quick glance up at the sign told them the road they were turning on was Shiloh.

Several nondescript houses sat opposite the field to their left. They were anonymous, weathered ranch style homes that were small, faded, and lacking in any sort of character. The yards were burnt in spots, scorched from the blazing sun and lack of water, while other patches were weed choked and overrun with tall grasses. There were cars in a couple of driveways and one with both doors hanging wide open. It was an old Dodge Aspen that looked half devoured with rust. Jason spotted what looked like a human skeleton, or part of one, wedged underneath the car, the legs only partially sticking out. Other than that there were no signs anyone had ever lived in the area.

"Clean as a whistle. Looks like no stiffs to deal with here. Nice." Jeff said as they came to the dirt path that would lead them to their goal.

As they turned he was surprised to find a small amount of water in several deep ruts on the road and tried to recall the last time it had rained. It was no more than a filmy muck and he navigated around a couple of the potholes that looked deep enough to bottom the van out.

Telephone poles were strung on the north side of the lane and the wires led directly to a modest house on the property. It looked to be an unpainted cottage with a single window facing their direction. Overall, the property looked well tended. Next to the house was a small whitewashed shed with its doors hanging open. Behind the two buildings was a grain silo. That was what had drawn Jeff's eye to the property in the first place. It soared above the house and was hard to miss. A few trees dotted the landscape, looming like leafy guardians in contrast to the emptiness of the surrounding fields. A rusted out tractor out back put the finishing touches on the quaint scene.

The van began its journey down the rutted road and Jeff guided it past the craters that could knock it out of commission. As they got closer they spotted a few more details that took away from the Norman Rockwell look of the place. The first was a BMX bike leaning up against the house and what appeared to be a hurriedly constructed grave marker next to it.

The van inched closer and everyone stared at the wooden cross. It was two pieces of plywood wrapped in twine and painted with illegible symbols across the horizontal board. Jeff squinted in an attempt to read the wording. The paint had run and it was hard to know for sure, but he guessed the letters spelled out a name. The other board looked as if it had been hastily jammed into the ground and had a slight lean to it.

Everyone was still focused on the cross when a man stepped out from behind the shed pointing a hunting rifle at them. Megan let out a small gasp and Jeff slammed on the brakes. The two rear passengers, who had been leaning forward in their seats, lost their footing and slipped to the floor.

"What the-" was all George could get out from down on the floor before Jeff cut him off.

"Stay down!" He hissed through gritted teeth. He wanted to follow his own command and duck beneath the dashboard, but the hunting rifle was trained on him. Instead, he carefully shifted the van into park and slowly raised his hands.

Out of the corner of his eye he saw Megan holding the revolver but she had not raised it above the dash just yet. He could sense more than see that she was waiting for something, perhaps a signal from him, to make a move. Jeff shook his head slightly. She carefully lowered the big hand gun down between her legs and clamped them shut around it. When she raised her own hands a small stitch of tension went out of Jeff.

"Both of you stay down. I don't think he saw you."

Jeff was no ventriloquist, but did his best to speak without moving his lips. The command was met with silence. He blinked away the sweat creeping into his eyes and stared at the man outside the van standing motionless in front of them.

The rifle had a scope attached to it and as far as Jeff could tell it was not of the bolt action variety. There was a clip coming out of the bottom and while he didn't know much about rifles, he guessed that meant it was a semi-automatic. In other words, it was time to play nice.

The man with the rifle motioned for him to get out of the van; short jabs pointing to the door. He was a good twenty feet away but that was close enough for Jeff's tastes.

"Stay in here," he mumbled as he reached for the door handle and lifted it. The door popped open and he began to slowly slide out.

"What do you want us to do?" George hissed from behind the driver's seat. He had gotten back up to his knees but heeded Jeff's command and was tucked out of sight. Jason was next to him, trying to sneak a peek around Megan's chair.

"If he shoots me, get the fuck out of here."

George felt like cursing or at the very least responding

with a sarcastic comment of his own, but Jeff was already shutting the door behind him. George reached under the console where he had spied a small lever and tugged at it. The small plastic cup holder fell flat to the side of Megan's seat and the small amount of junk on it, including a map Jeff had marked up, fell to the floor. Now he had a small passage to the front seats if he could squirm his way up there without being seen.

"Shit, he wants me out there too. What do I do?"

George didn't know if Megan's question was rhetorical or not but decided to answer.

"Leave that gun of yours on the seat and I'll think of something. And *be* careful."

Megan risked a glance down at George. The fear on her face told him how badly she did not want to go outside. There were tears welling up in her eyes but she nodded slightly. As she opened the door and began to move George slid his hand up and grabbed her arm gently, giving it a quick squeeze. She froze for a moment and then started moving again, allowing the gun to fall between her legs onto the seat. George let go of Megan's arm and quickly discovered the warm metal of the .357 Magnum beneath his fingers.

Outside, Jeff was attempting to start a conversation with the man he hoped wasn't planning on killing them.

"Hello! Are we glad to see you! We haven't seen anyone living in quite-"

"Shut the fuck up and show me your hands."

Jeff raised his hands higher. His captor kept the rifle trained on him but gave Megan a long hard look as she dropped down from the van and came out from behind the open door. She pushed it shut slowly and moved forward, her hands above her head as well.

"Look, I know things are screwed up but there's no reason to point a rifle at us. We don't want any trouble," Jeff pleaded.

"Ya, right. Everyone is trouble these days. I'm not taking any chances."

Jeff tensed slightly at the comment and took a closer look at the man who had ambushed them. His tone of voice was cynical but not sinister and he certainly didn't look like some sort of bandit.

He had on expensive loafers and a pair of dirty black designer jeans. If that was not enough, the alligator logo on his shirt confirmed he wasn't some farmer trying to ward poachers off his land. His reddish blond thinning hair was an unkempt mess and the bags under his eyes testified to the fact that he had suffered through many sleepless nights lately. Looking soft and somewhat round, it was clear that the man toting the rifle had not endured much in the form of hardship throughout most of his life. At least not until the plague had come along and spoiled everything. Jeff knew he was looking at a desperate scavenger, and nothing more.

"Move away from the van. Come toward me, slowly...okay, stop there." Jeff and Megan were about ten feet in front of the grill of the minivan and about twice the distance from their yuppie captor, who had backpedaled as they came forward.

"Look, Mister...?" Megan said in a timid voice. She could see the man in front of them was nervous, his eyes darting back and forth between her and Jeff. She inched forward slightly, hoping against hope she could talk their way out of this mess.

The rifle swung in her direction. She froze and felt her legs go numb.

"Bitch, shut the FUCK up and stay right where you are!"

The man's grip on the rifle tightened and despite the residue of nervousness about him he was able to keep it pointed directly at her heart.

"Hey man! Take it easy! We don't have any weapons." Jeff shouted, hoping to turn the attention back to him and away from Megan.

He got his wish and suddenly Jeff was staring down the barrel of the rifle once again.

"I told you to both to SHUT UP! I meant it. I don't wanna have to kill you!"

Jeff could hear panic in the words. The urban "warrior" holding the expensive rifle on them was sweating profusely and blinking like crazy. As his eyes danced back and forth between his two prisoners, Jeff began to worry about the man's mental stability.

After a few moments their captor calmed down enough to look past them toward the van. Inching to his right to see around Jeff and Megan, he scanned the vehicle with an appraising eye.

The Odyssey had seen better days. It looked like it was getting ready for the demolition derby. The windshield was still in one piece but there were several growing spider web cracks in it. Deep gouges ran along the sides, the front was dented to hell, and the grill had snapped in several places. One of the headlights outer casings had shattered and there were splatters of blackened goop in most of the available nooks and crannies. An attempt to clear away the spray of blood and chunks of flesh on the windshield had done little more than create a smeared haze. It was a mess.

"Anyone else in there?" the man holding them prisoner asked Jeff. When he didn't get an immediate response he continued. "You better tell me right now if you know what's good for you...*all* of you. ANYONE IN THERE?" His eyes didn't leave Jeff as he threw the question toward the van. "COME ON OUT NOW AND EVERYTHING'LL BE OKAY."

The scavenger suddenly smiled, trying to show he could be good natured if need be.

"Bobby?" He leaned his head back slightly as he spoke, throwing his words behind him.

"Yah, dad?"

The voice came from the house. Jeff looked toward the structure and saw that the front door was wide open. A young man stood there with another rifle pointed at him. At first glance it looked like he was a teenager and there was no doubt he was the man's son. Get rid of the round gut and thinning hair the older man had and they were spitting images of one another. Bobby held his rifle in a relaxed stance as he squinted down the sight. His did not have a scope but Jeff could see he had a bead on him. The boy did not move away from the doorframe even after his father called to him, preferring to remain close to cover.

Jeff gritted his teeth and cursed under his breath. Things were getting worse by the minute.

"You got them covered?"

"No prob, dad."

"Good boy."

The father's smile grew larger. His nervousness had diminished greatly. He nodded toward his son but stared at Jeff as his voice dropped down to a near whisper. "My boy's a good shot-a hell of a lot better than me. He used to hunt with his uncles *all* the time." The father moved closer and looked at Jeff conspiratorially. "Now I might be a little nervous about shooting you, but Bobby there...well, if I tell him to shoot, he'll do it, no questions asked."

More teeth were displayed as the crooked grin got even wider. "Now, you *do* believe me, don't you?"

Jeff stared at the father and then past him to the son, whose rifle was still pointed at his head. He nodded.

"Good. Then we understand one another."

The man took a step back and his chest swelled. He took another look at the van.

"Now I'm gonna to ask just one more time. Is there anyone else in there?"

Jeff took a deep breath and held it for a moment before letting it out slowly. He smiled, matching his opponent's grin tooth for tooth. His confidence elevated slightly when he saw the brave façade on the other man's face start to crack. Making his decision in that split second, he shook his head in denial.

"You better not be fucking with me. You do realize that, don't you?"

Jeff continued to grin.

After another few seconds of staring at Jeff, Bobby's father looked at the van again. He squinted at it, a curious look on his face.

"So what've you got in there? Food? Water?"

"Uh huh. Medicine too. All kinds of stuff."

Jeff's head swiveled over to Megan and his grin faltered.

"We could share it with you."

Now both men were looking at her, their eyes growing wide with surprise.

"Please, we could help each other out!" Megan sounded desperate and excited as Jeff began to silently fume beside her. "If we give you some of our food and medicine you could let us stay here tonight." Suddenly, she was on a roll and seemed to forget all about the gun pointed at her. "I think we should stick together instead of fighting one another. We won't cause you any trouble, I swear to God! We just want a place to rest and then we'll move on. It'll be like we were never here at all...except you'll have a lot more food for you, your son, and whoever else is with you."

Jeff watched their captor's expression and his hopes rose when it appeared he actually seemed to be considering Megan's offer. At least that seemed to be the case until she spoke her last few words. Then, it was as if a switch had been flipped and his face suddenly contorted in rage.

"Lady, my son and I are alone and we intend to keep it that way. We don't need anyone else screwing things up for us. We survived this long without any outsiders and we sure as hell don't need you hanging around causing us even more grief than we've already suffered through." He shook his head in contempt. "Shit, you probably drew enough attention with your goddamn van to wake up every one of those fucking bastards in a three mile radius."

"No! No! Listen, we-"

The man raised his voice, ignoring Megan's protests. "So my son and I are gonna let you deal with whatever shit you stirred up. That minivan of yours is our ticket outta here."

"No! You can't take the van!"

"Shut up Megan!" Jeff jumped in before she could provoke the man toting the rifle any further. Jeff shook his head and glared at her, a rabid expression on his face. Megan's mouth slammed shut and she took a step back.

"Look...can you please tell us your name at least?" Jeff turned back to the man, the words flying out of his mouth as he tried desperately to regain control of the situation.

"You don't need to know what my name is, pal. Once my son and I leave it'll be the last you'll ever see of us."

"So it shouldn't matter, right? Look, I know your son's name and let's face it; we're not going to have an APB put out on you, are we? I just want to know who I'm dealing with." Jeff had regained his composure enough to try another smile, this one a bit meeker than before.

The man holding them prisoner stared hard at Jeff and started to say something but stopped himself. He rolled his eyes and lowered the gun slightly as he made a noise that sounded like a frustrated laugh. Jeff tried to inject even more warmth into his smile.

"Dad? What're you doing?"

Jeff could tell from Bobby's voice that he was starting to get nervous, just like his father.

"It's under control son, just relax and keep your pants on!" Dad said, his frustration starting to wear on him.

He looked at Jeff again and sighed. "The name's Fred, for all the good it'll do ya."

Jeff increased the wattage of his smile. "Well Fred, my name's Jeff. This is my wife, Megan."

He held his breathe and prayed Megan would play along. When she didn't stare at him in surprise Jeff relaxed slightly. All he knew was that he had to keep stalling and try to give Fred enough of a reason to feel guilty about what he was doing.

"I can't believe we've made it this far. We somehow managed to get out of town after everything fell apart. Those things were all over us. Honestly, I'm just glad to be here." Jeff looked over at Megan affectionately. She seemed a bit disoriented from his lie but smiled disjointedly back at him. He started inching closer to her until the rifle began to elevate once again. Jeff held up his hands in appeasement and stopped.

"Yeh, yeh, whatever," Fred remarked irritably. "I'm gonna take a look at the van. We want to be out of the area by nightfall. You and your wife can jaw all you want about how you escaped the city after we're gone." He started moving toward the van.

"Where's *your* wife, Fred?"

When Fred stiffened and the color disappeared from his face, Jeff knew he had struck a nerve. He hadn't had an idea what he was going to say until the words tumbled out of his mouth. Something had been gnawing at him since he had stepped out of the van and now he realized what it was.

"Is that her grave?" Jeff pointed to the marker they had seen driving up to the property: the makeshift cross and the freshly turned dirt. The disturbed earth was long and wide enough for an adult to be buried underneath it.

"Is that Bobby's mother?"

"Shut up." It was a growled threat.

Jeff kept pressing. "I'm just wondering, because we had to bury two children back in Milfield. They got bit, got the plague, and we had to watch them die, Fred. So I was just curious if you might understand what we've been dealing with."

"SHUT UP GOD DAMMIT!" Fred was screaming but his eyes were closed as he pointed the rifle like a spear at Jeff's chest.

"Dad, what's wrong?!"

Bobby was finally moving off the porch toward them. He was almost running and still trying to point the rifle at the two prisoners. He stopped a few feet away but Jeff could see the agitation on his face. Like his father he was taller than average but still growing into his body. Back on the porch, he looked like he meant business. Up close, even with a rifle in his hands he looked like nothing more than a confused kid.

Fred almost turned to face his son but held his position and glared at Jeff. "Get the hell back to the porch! NOW!" Bobby hovered for a couple of moments before reluctantly backing up.

Jeff kept the look of misery on his face. The bluff he was trying to pull off was far too close to the truth for him to not feel some of the pain he was projecting.

"Fred, please. We're just trying to survive here. We've already seen way too much death. Haven't you?" He leaned forward slightly as hate burned in the other man's eyes. "Why don't we help each other out so we can all get out of here together?"

The butt of the rifle connected with his jaw so quickly that Jeff barely saw it coming. Fred had been moving closer ever since Jeff started talking but when he leaned forward he presented an irresistible target. There was no pain as he fell to the ground-the clipped scream of surprise from Megan was the first thing he noticed after nearly getting his jaw dislocated.

It rattled his teeth and knocked him flat but as Jeff moved his hand up to his jaw he wasn't quite sure what had happened. When the pain finally came a few seconds later it started as a dull throb.

"Stay away from him you asshole!" Megan scrambled to Jeff's side, grabbing him around the shoulders and shielding him from any further attacks. Fred was done though. He stepped back, his rage sated for the moment. He looked more confused than ever and the reprimand from Megan seemed to give him pause.

"Bastard."

The expletive was whispered as Megan examined Jeff's jaw, touching the fast rising welt delicately. His head moved back quickly after her fingers hit the raw spot and he sucked in air through his teeth. She relaxed slightly when she realized his jaw wasn't broken.

Megan looked up at Fred. Her eyes were hot flares that burned straight through him. He stepped back, giving her the chance to help Jeff, first to his knees and then his feet. He gingerly rubbed his jaw as he glared at Fred, who was too busy looking at the van again to care.

"Where's the keys? Give 'em to me."

"Fred-"

"I'm tired of this shit! That IS my wife over there and I was the one who had to put her down! Satisfied? Happy to know I had to deal with the same shit you did, you fucking prick?" Fred's eyes were full of fire as he spoke. "In about two seconds, if you don't hand over those keys I swear to God I'll be digging two more holes!"

The rifle was in Jeff's face again, but this time he could see no doubt on Fred's visage. The ruse had backfired and there was nothing else to do. Eyes darting quickly over to Bobby, Jeff saw that the boy's rifle was pointed in their direction but his eyes were glued to his father.

"Keys are in the ignition." Jeff grimaced at the pain speaking caused his jaw. He leaned against Megan, still a bit woozy from the blow.

"Stay here," Fred commanded. "Bobby? Don't let them out of your sight! I'm checking out the van."

"Okay dad." Bobby sounded nervous, almost depressed, but the gun remained elevated and his eyes focused on the two clinging figures thirty feet in front of him.

Jeff waited until Fred had walked away before he whispered in Megan's ear. "Get ready."

She stiffened and looked him in the eyes. Nodding almost imperceptibly, Megan tensed. She knew George had her gun.

Fred moved to the van. He glared at Jeff one last time, not bothering to say anything as he pointed his weapon at the vehicle. Moving in, he glanced quickly through the tinted windows behind the driver's door. He looked closer for a moment. Satisfied, he inched up and stared inside. There were the keys, dangling from the ignition, just as Jeff had said. He did not see anyone, just a jumble of boxes and other crap strewn about, as if the minivan had been through an earthquake.

Fred allowed himself a small grin as he moved the rifle to his left hand and pointed it skyward. Opening the door, he leaned in. The keys were pushed into the ignition completely and the van started chirping in annoyance. He twisted the key and the engine turned over. The idle was a quiet purr and gas needle bounced from empty to almost full...a smidge below. His grin widened.

The thrill lasted less than a second before he heard a distinct *click*.

Fred froze, his rifle pointed straight up and inconveniently was still outside the vehicle, along with his left arm. His head, chest, and right arm were completely exposed. He slowly turned his head at a downward angle and confirmed there was a handgun pointed at his face.

George was sprawled on the floor, a blanket covering him except for the top of his head and the barrel of the gun, which was pointed at Fred.

"Drop the rifle. DON'T move your head or even twitch a muscle."

It came out in a hiss. The man above him was glaring down with a mixture of anger and resentment. George returned the look.

Fred paused for a moment, taking a deep breath. He looked like he was thinking over George's command when he saw a head pop up from behind the second row of seats. Jason was holding Jeff's gore stained baseball bat.

"You better do as he says."

"Jason! Get down. NOW!" George commanded. The boy kept his eyes on Fred as he ducked down slightly so he could still peak over the seat.

Fred dropped the rifle and raised his hands, leaning out of the van but moving slowly. He continued to stare at Jason as George spoke to him.

"Now call off your pal out there. Do it! I want our

friends safe and sound back inside the van."

Fred stared down at the .357 Magnum. The look on his face made it clear he most definitely did not want to do as he was being told. He began to turn away from the van but stopped quickly as the gun rose up and the boy in the back of the vehicle began to move forward. Looking at both of them, Fred seemed to change his mind.

"Bobby! Go back in the house and lock the door. Do it now." There was not much enthusiasm in the command.

"Daddy?" Bobby looked at his father but his rifle never left Jeff and Megan.

Fred looked at his son, his voice deflated. "Just do it, son. Get back in the house."

Bobby just stared at his father, his mouth wide open and his eyes blinking rapidly. He started slowly moving off the porch.

Fred turned toward his son, forgetting the gun pointed at him for a moment as anger colored his face. "Robert Charles Harrington! Get your ass back in that house right this minute!" Bobby froze and stared for a moment before his eyes turned to Jeff and Megan.

The hope Jeff had that things might actually turn out okay disappeared the instant he saw the look on Bobby's face.

The kid moved toward him. The rifle was aimed at his head and didn't waver.

Jeff shoved Megan behind him as the boy moved closer. Bobby was within three feet but almost all of the remaining distance was covered by the barrel of his rifle. Megan saw Jeff's hands motioning for her to move away, to run; to do *something*.

Fred continued to yell at his son from where he stood next to the van, but it was clear to Jeff that Bobby had decided to take things into his own hands.

"Tell whoever's in the van to let my father go."

His voice was steady. Bobby kept ignoring his dad and pointed the rifle at Jeff's forehead.

Suddenly, Fred stopped yelling. He was still gawking

at his son, but his face had suddenly changed. He looked afraid.

"Bobby." The voice was as steady as he could make it, Fred's anger gone. "Bobby, *listen* to me. I made a mistake-a *big* mistake. I...I'm sorry son." Fred looked back into the van for a moment. "I'm really sorry. I shouldn't have done this. I didn't want to hurt anybody. You know that. I just wanted...I just wanted to find a way out of here."

The words got Bobby's attention. He kept the rifle pointed at Jeff but his eyes darted to his father. He was close enough to see the fear in his dad's eyes. His head cocked sideways and a look of confusion passed over his face.

Just then, the passenger door on the Odyssey opened. Bobby's eyes moved away from his father and he saw the woman that had been creeping backwards getting into the van.

Suddenly, the confusion was gone. Bobby shifted the rifle and moved slightly to afford him a clear view of the van door that the woman was hiding behind.

Megan heard the sound of the rifle firing and a *thunk* following so closely it was simultaneous. She dropped to her knees behind the van door as she tried desperately to cover up. Looking up, she saw a small hole had appeared in the door. A second shot was fired and she dove inside the van.

Jeff had heard the van door open too. He could see the expression on Bobby's face and knew what the kid was going to do. When he moved the rifle Jeff tried to react immediately but couldn't. His feet felt stuck in place. The first shot jolted him but it took seeing Bobby throwing the bolt on the rifle and the empty cartridge flying free before he was able to lunge for the boy.

Bobby saw him coming and tried to level the rifle at him. The second shot went wild as they tumbled to the ground. Jeff grabbed for the weapon and got a single hand on it as Bobby's knee came up. They landed awkwardly, with Jeff twisting to the side slightly. The blow knocked the wind out of him but he had avoided the knee to his crotch. Even with the pain of the attack he managed to keep his hand tight on the rifle, even as the boy tried to wrench it free.

When George heard the van door open behind him he shifted, fearful it was the other gunman. That was all Fred needed. He started running toward his son as Bobby fired the first shot. George heard it as well and then saw Megan dive in the van directly above him. He was relieved it was her but was already in a panic at having lost sight of Fred. He began trying to dislodge himself from his cramped position between the two chairs. As he did, he heard the distinct sound of one of the minivan's side doors opening in its slow, methodical way. More sunlight beamed into the cargo area but a shadow blotted it out for a moment before it was bright again. Panic jarred him and he began struggling even harder. He started to yell but it was already too late.

"Jason! No!"

Fred wasn't thinking about his lost rifle as he reached the spot where Jeff and Bobby were fighting. He lashed out with his foot and landed a grazing blow to the back of Jeff's head, which snapped forward. Jeff crumpled to the ground. He was barely conscious as he let go of the rifle and put his hands over his skull to shield it from further blows. Bobby was pushing him away and Fred helped drag the boy out from underneath the bleeding man. Jeff rolled over onto his back, a dazed look on his face. Bobby scooted back as his father grabbed the rifle away from him.

Fred quickly pointed the weapon down at Jeff. He had a sad look on his face.

"Fred?" Jeff's eyes were blurry and he wasn't sure who was standing over him. He tried to prop himself up on one elbow but suddenly felt dizzy and couldn't manage it. "Fred, is that you?" The words were slurred, as if he were drunk.

Fred put the rifle butt up against his shoulder. "I'm sorry Jeff. But no one attacks my boy." He lined up the sights and slipped his finger into the trigger guard as he took a deep breath.

The world exploded. Jeff was trying to say "*no*" to the man he thought might be Fred when the man's entire left side disappeared. He bucked forward and a gout of blood burst from his chest. There were a couple of screams: one filled with anguish, the other more pitiful. Suddenly the man was falling.

George finally wrestled free of the captain's chairs and was face to face with Megan.

"Give me the gun!" She shouted and he tossed it to her as he moved out the door Jason had just left through. He had not seen where the boy went but heard the shot ring out so close that it felt like his eardrums would burst. He went cold at the sound.

George stepped out of the van and saw Jason standing there, the rifle Fred had dropped in his hands, the end of the barrel smoking.

"Jason? Jason, what happened?" George felt a sickening dread wash over him as he looked past the boy. When he saw Fred's bleeding body he stumbled backwards.

"Oh my God, what have you done?!"

He turned away from the gruesome image and looked at Jason again. The twelve year old was still staring in the direction the man he had shot but his eyes were blank. He legs began to wobble and George rushed up to catch him as let go of the rifle. Jason looked at him with dull eyes and did not seem to recognize the man he had spent the last month with. George suppressed a shiver and pulled the boy close, hugging him tightly as he began pulling him toward the van. He heard someone starting to scream behind him.

"Dad?"

Bobby, who had been on the ground watching his father, began crawling over to where Fred had fallen. The entry wound was small on his back and he hoped it was minor. The bullet had pierced his father below the shoulder and plowed into his left lung. The teen touched the wound and pulled his fingers back as if stung.

"Daddy?!" Frantically, he rolled his father over, only to discover a massive exit wound. It was hard to tell how big the hole was with all the blood pouring out. Bobby slapped his hand over it, desperately trying to staunch the flow but Fred's left lung had already collapsed. There were a few short wheezes as the last of the sticky liquid gushed out of his chest.

Bobby's scream coincided with the final shuttering breath of his father. He lifted Fred in his arms and wailed in agony. He raised his head and looked back at the van. In an instant, he was standing, his father's blood smeared across his shirt and pants.

"YOU! You fucking bastards! You murdered my daddy!"

He spotted George and Jason and saw his father's rifle at their feet. He reached toward his belt and undid the snap holding his hunting knife. Pulling the large blade out, he began walking toward them. As they moved inside the van he began to run, the knife clutched in his raised hand.

"Bobby!"

He barely heard his name being called and ignored it as he picked up speed. He was almost to the van.

"Bobby, stop! I don't want to shoot you!"

He howled as he raised his weapon above his head. His eyes were trained on George's back.

Megan's first shot spun Bobby sideways but he didn't feel it. He staggered but righted himself, his eyes never leaving his target. Her second shot went wild, missing him by a foot. He began to move forward again when she pulled the trigger for the third time. Teeth and shards of bone disintegrated as the .357 slug tore through his jaw. Bobby's head twisted sharply away from his body and he collapsed to the ground.

Shaking violently, Megan rounded the van and kept the gun pointed at the fallen boy. He had dropped his knife and his face was buried in the dirt. He shuddered spasmodically and then went still.

Megan stared down at Bobby, watching his blood form a distorted halo around his head before the dry ground began absorbing the liquid. She stared at him for a few more seconds, wiping a bitter tear from her eye before she moved to where George was comforting Jason inside the van.

"Could you help me with Jeff? We need to get out of here."

George looked at her and nodded. The dullness in her eyes was far too familiar; it was the same look Jason had.

He did his best to ignore the bodies; especially the young boy's. He strode purposefully past the first corpse, his eyes locked on Jeff's prone form. Fred's torn body was next to him. The smell of coppery blood was overpowering and George had to turn away and bend over to quell his rebellious stomach.

When Megan spoke from directly behind him George felt like jumping twenty feet straight up. "Can you get Jeff? He's too heavy for me and I'm going to get the rifles and any bullets they had." Megan shoved the hand gun into her pocket as George stared back at her with confusion in his eyes.

"George?" She touched him delicately on the shoulder and he recoiled. Her dead eyed stare had diminished and Megan was registering concern for him but he was still trying to comprehend what she had just done.

"It's-I'm okay. No, really, I am. I just...I just need a minute." He stuttered and stumbled his way through the words. It appeared to placate her.

Jeff came to much more easily than George thought he would. He had been clocked pretty good but the bleeding had stopped. He asked about Megan so George gave him a shorthand account of what had happened. Jeff was too dazed to react but seemed to understand. He got to his feet with George's help and they climbed into the back of the van, where Jason sat quietly.

Megan forced herself to do a quick search of the two bodies. She did not move them, but patted their pockets and found a few rounds of ammunition but not much else. She looked over at the small house but decided not to bother with it.

She walked the perimeter of the van, shutting the doors and settling in behind the steering wheel. Everyone else was in the back seats. Megan glanced over at the bullet hole in the passenger door and studied it for a moment before looking out the window.

"I guess all that noise stirred up the neighbors."

George leaned over to look out the windows. Off in the distance, closing in from various directions, were several staggering figures. The shots had woken them from their slumber, or whatever it was that they did when no one was around to irritate them.

Some were closer than others, coming from the direction of the houses and even through the dense woods to the north. Further off, from the opposite direction, there were more making their slow and determined march toward the cottage.

"Should we bury the bodies...?" Megan asked.

George shook his head. "It would be the decent thing to do, even though...but no, there's no point. I think they could still smell them and I wouldn't put it past them to dig up a body-especially if it's...fresh."

They watched the slowly approaching shapes for a few more seconds before George spoke again.

"Let's just go."

Megan looked at him through the rear view mirror. "Wanna sit next to me?"

She could see the discomfort her question caused. "Nah, I think I'll stay back here with these two and make sure they're okay." Megan nodded quickly and shifted the van into drive.

"Sounds good."

Sitting alone as she drove past the grasping arms

reaching out for them, Megan didn't look back as she turned onto the main road.

After a few moments she felt relieved that George had rejected her offer to sit up front as she began to cry silently.

Chapter 21

Megan kept driving east. Sticking with the road they were on would lead them to Manchester, the next town on the map. She did not relish the idea of getting near another town of any size, even if it wasn't part of the suburban sprawl like Milfield or Gallatin, so she began looking for another place they could hunker down for the night.

Her tears dried as rows of corn flowed by the van. There was a mix of gravel and asphalt routes leading off to obscure back roads between the crops. Manchester was straight ahead, less than five miles away and looming on the horizon.

"Eeny, meeney, miney, mo..." she mumbled.

Taking a left down a random road, she didn't bother looking at the sign that told her its name. They were surrounded by crops taller than the van with a thin strip of asphalt heading off into the distance.

Megan saw a smaller gravel lane creeping up on them and slowed to study it. For no real reason she turned right and headed down the rough path. On the passenger side crops went on to the horizon but on Megan's side of the road she could see them cutting off, maybe a mile or less from where they were.

"Where are we going?" Jeff asked from the back seat, his voice slightly slurred.

"Just trying to find us someplace for the night," Megan

tossed over her shoulder.

As the corn stalks fell away trees took their place. Split rail fencing surrounding someone's land popped up and the trees continued behind it. After a hundred feet there was a break and a long driveway split off through a large yard. Megan stared down the path and saw a modest farmhouse. It was old and rustic looking with a grassy expanse surrounding it that was huge-at least three or four acres. The grass had grown wild but it was obvious the place had been cared for. Large, mature trees populated the yard and woodlands dropped off behind the house. The gravel drive hit the traditional two story house at the attached garage. A tire swing was off to the left and an above ground pool set back in the giant backyard.

"So is this where we're staying tonight?" George inquired.

Megan looked back at him. He was sitting between Jeff and Jason, ostensibly to tend to both of them. "Not sure," she said, and looked back at the house. "It looks okay, doesn't it?"

"Looks fine to me, let's check it out."

Megan kept staring at the house. It was far back from the road. The property line ran for a good distance. They were surrounded by farmland and it was relatively remote. Still, she felt some doubt.

"Megan?"

She ignored George as she kept scouring the landscape and house with her eyes, watching for movement. After a few seconds she looked down at the fuel gauge. They had plenty of gas to keep moving, but where could they go that would be any better than this?

Sighing, she moved the van forward until there were several large trees between it and the house before she shut off the engine. Reaching over, she grabbed her revolver. Opening the door, she stepped outside.

The cargo door was opening as well and George stepped out holding one of the rifles. He looked toward the house as he spoke. "Let's go have a look."

Megan stepped in front of him. He stood over her and sunlight beamed down from behind him, casting Megan in shadow. She shook her head as she shoved the hand gun into the waistband of her pants. "I can do this by myself. I need you to stay here and watch those two," she said as she waved her hand at the open van door.

George looked indignant but had the decency to hide it behind a forced smile. He kept it there as he did his best to look confident and tough, but Megan could see how awkward the rifle looked in his hands.

"Megan, you can't do this alone. Come on! We can scope this place out and if there's trouble we'll back each other up." His sickly grin got even wider and he moved a step closer. "In fact, if anyone should be staying here, it should be you. I'll go and you stay here to keep an eye out for any trouble."

Megan stared up at him with a smile on her face that did not reach her eyes. George was nearly a foot taller than her but she did not look intimidated. When she stepped closer, his smile faltered and he backed up slightly.

"George, I don't think that's a good idea. In fact, I think it's a lousy idea." Her smile disappeared suddenly and her demeanor became stern.

"I'm going up to that house and I am going to make sure no one is there. If there are any of those things, I'll shoot them. If there are any people, I'll try to reason with them but if that doesn't work I'll do what I have to, whatever that may be. Is any of this unclear to you?"

"Megan, I-"

"No George, I don't want to hear it. There's no time for any macho-man bullshit right now, okay? I'm tired, hungry, and can't deal with your BS on top of everything else."

The intensity in Megan's eyes made George want to take another step back but he rocked on his heels instead.

"Look, I'm sorry, it's just that..." he sputtered.

"Forget it George. We can argue later about who should do what but for right now I don't want to worry about hurt feelings, alright? I just want to get this over with and the longer I stand here the grouchier I get." She stomped past him, bumping his arm as she did. He staggered back slightly even though there was no way her slight frame could have moved him. George turned to watch her walk toward the entrance of the property, a look of stunned confusion on his face.

"Let her go."

George turned to look at Jeff, who had his seat lying back and his arms behind his head. "She's gonna do whatever she wants and I doubt there's much you can do to stop her."

George looked back at Megan and sighed.

Jeff propped himself up on his elbows. "Megan was a basket case when I first met her. That was only yesterday."

George stared at him, his eyes narrowing in confusion at the comment.

"Yeah, I know. It doesn't seem possible," Jeff said with a knowing smile. "But as you can see, things have changed. Our little Megan has grown up fast." He winced as he gingerly rubbed his jaw. He chuckled and shook his head slightly. "I bet her husband had fun dealing with her when she was angry."

He shifted and put his hands behind his head again as he laid back on the seat.

George stared at him and then gritted his teeth in frustration and flopped down in the open doorway of the van. He glanced at Jason and saw that the boy was ignoring the conversation as he stared blankly out his window.

Turning back toward the house, he could no longer see Megan. The rifle felt strange in his hands but he still wanted to jump up and go after her. His heart raced as he felt torn between taking off and guarding Jeff and Jason, who weren't in the best shape at the moment.

After what seemed like forever but was in reality only a couple of minutes, George stood up. He had resisted interfering for as long as possible. With the rifle in hand he began moving away from the van. He knew Jeff and Jason had the other rifle to defend themselves with. That along with the fact that he had heard nothing more ominous than the wind blowing was enough to convince him that he needed to help Megan whether she liked it or not.

"I'm gonna go see what's taking her so long," he tossed behind him as he skirted the trees they had parked behind. He came around them and stopped short.

Megan was standing on the porch with the front door open behind her, waving at him.

Megan had searched the outside and inside of the house once she discovered the back door was unlocked. It looked like it had been abandoned weeks before, with many of the possessions of the family that had lived there gone. The garaged revealed only some dried out oil spots where their vehicles had once sat but the pantry was stocked with all kinds of canned and dry goods. She didn't attempt to open the refrigerator, knowing whatever was inside had gone bad long ago. The rest of the house looked to be in good order.

There were four bedrooms, which thrilled everyone to no end. Reasonably fresh sheets were in the linen closet and George and Megan gleefully set to changing the beds. Jason snapped out of his daze a bit during this process and "claimed" one of the rooms that had obviously been a teenager's.

Megan played nurse and tended to Jeff's bruises. There was little she could do for his jaw with no ice but bandaged his scalp, stinging his cuts with peroxide. After a quick examination of George and Jason, Megan pronounced they were all in good health with no outstanding wounds or infections to concern themselves with.

They agreed to have dinner together after checking out the barbeque grill and finding the propane tank half full. No steaks but George insisted he could do something interesting with the Spam and Pork and Beans they found on one of the shelves.

They discovered with some surprise that there was still water pressure and realized that the property had its own well and a generator in the basement. None of them had the knowledge to get the dusty old machine running but found several large containers they filled with water.

They pulled the van into the garage and began loading it up with the loot they had found in the house. Jeff was feeling less woozy and took charge of the task, dumping as much as he could into the rear of the van.

There was no heat so each of them took a quick and invigorating cold shower and then ransacked the place for clean clothes. A sizeable collection of books were picked through and several were put in a small cardboard box. When they sat down to dinner on the deck a couple of hours later they felt exhausted but happy.

"It's been a hell of a day, hasn't it?" Jeff leaned back in his plastic lawn chair as he stretched out, lacing his fingers behind his bandaged head.

"Well, if that ain't the understatement of the century." Megan jabbed him in the ribs with her elbow and they all shared a quiet laugh.

"So now what?"

They all stared off into space as Jeff's question hung in the air.

"I'm not asking for a big picture answer guys, just asking what we should do next." Jeff paused, staring at his empty plate. "I mean, you know what I want to do."

The pause became awkward as Jeff, then Megan, and finally Jason began looking at George. He could feel their eyes burning into him as he looked down at his hands.

"I can't ask you to help me get to my family. I know it'll be dangerous. But *I* need to get back to them. I think...I think I want to find a car and head back home on my own."

There was defiance on George's face as he looked up. His eyes moved to Megan as she leaned over the table toward him.

She tried to smile but couldn't. "We understand George. We won't try to stop you when you decide to go."

Her smile did come then, but was not confident or strong. She held her hand out to George and he stared at it. His face was full of relief as he blinked slowly and took her tiny hand in his oversized paw. When George looked over at Jeff he was nodding in agreement. There was a hint of regret in his eyes but it disappeared quickly.

George's smile faltered slightly when he glanced at Jason. The boy was trying his hardest to look disinterested in the conversation as he picked at the food remaining on his plate.

Jason had always been hard for George to read. From the time they were thrust together in the high school gymnasium, alongside hundreds of other refugees, to their endless days stuck inside the church, the kid had shared little about himself. Their isolation had nearly driven George mad as he thought about and prayed for his family constantly. Jason, on the other hand, remained stoic and distant and didn't seem to mind that they were trapped. All George knew about him was that he had lost his mother, a single parent, during the first few days of the plague. That was it. The rest of Jason's story remained a mystery. That seemed to be the way the kid liked it.

The quartet fell into silence, the burning question of the moment answered. They sat back and relaxed, enjoying the sound of the slight breeze whispering through the trees and the crickets off in the distance.

After a while, Jeff sat up in his chair and clapped his hands together. Everyone looked at him.

"Well, enough of this lounging around and doing nothing crap. Let's see if we can find a deck of cards or a board game in this mausoleum and have some fun."

Megan grinned and went into the house. A few minutes later she was back with a stack of games she had found in a closet. They decided on Monopoly and for the next hour or so, until the sun started dipping down in the west, they rolled the dice and laughed with one other.

They moved a couple of sofas from the family room in front of the French doors at the back of the house and the dining room table and chairs were stacked in front of the main entrance. They knew the neither of the makeshift barriers would hold up if they came under assault but they would decide if they should make the defenses more permanent or just move on in the morning.

As they climbed the steps to the bedrooms Megan was nervous about Jeff's head injuries, fearing he had a concussion. He laughed it off but she insisted he not fall asleep if that was the case. Exhausted, he was prepared to argue with her until George stepped in and offered to stay up with Jeff. They would stand watch from up in one of the bedrooms. When he winked at Jeff as Megan was looking elsewhere, Jeff agreed quickly and the matter was settled.

The two men took the rifles and chose a bedroom with a view of the front lawn. They scrounged up a card table and chairs and started playing cards by moonlight.

"I'm okay, George, really," Jeff said as they settled in.

George nodded. "I know." He smiled as he looked over at other man. "I saw plenty of concussions back in my football days and you don't have any of the symptoms."

He leaned forward and gave Jeff a conspiratorial look. "But as you said, Megan is going to do whatever she wants and there's not much you can do to stop her."

He winked and a grin cracked Jeff's face as he snorted with laughter.

"You got that right," he agreed.

"So I figured we would play some cards, shoot the bull, and then take turns sleeping."

Jeff nodded. "Setting up watch ain't such a bad idea anyway."

George just smiled as he began shuffling the deck.

As they relaxed and started to play, they began to chat

about their lives.

George was happy to talk about his wife Helen and two daughters, Roxanne, who was twelve, and Debra, eight. They had lived in Wildwood, a suburb of Dayton, for the last ten years, ever since George had gone back to college to get a degree after getting laid off by Ford. He was a programmer and worked on special projects all over the region.

"I was on a short one in Gallatin-only about three days worth of work, when they began quarantining the area." He shook his head in frustration. "It was an intense project: sixteen hour days so they can get you out of there quick. So I stayed in a hotel even though I'm less than an hour away..." He trailed off as he stared out the window at nothing.

After a few seconds of silence George realized he had stopped talking and looked down at his cards again.

"Anyway, I got hijacked by Guardsmen out of my hotel room and tossed into that pit." His lips puckered with distaste. "They packed us like sardines in that gym and when they ran out of space there they started cramming more people into the other schools.

"I tried to keep in touch with Helen but cell phone coverage was for shit and then died altogether."

Jeff nodded, recalling a conversation with his sister that had blinked out. It was just as she was telling him about some island off the coast of Washington state, where she lived, that her and her husband were going to try and wait things out on.

"The last time we spoke was when she agreed they would stay in the house. We have plenty of food and water in the basement." George looked at Jeff and smiled ruefully. "I like shopping in bulk at Sam's." Jeff returned the smile and nodded. The far off look came back into George's eyes. "So we agreed they would stay there. Cover the windows, put some boards over the doors, and wait for me to get back."

"So...what happened at the gym?" Jeff gently nudged George to continue when he stopped again.

"It was a massacre."

George relayed his story in short, choppy sentences. He had met Jason and a young married couple in the high school gym and they had clung to each other as everyone around them started going crazy. Rumors were rampant about what was happening in local cities like Cincinnati and Dayton and how everything was falling apart. It was falling apart inside the gym as well and it took everything the soldiers had to keep everyone under control. Stories of death squads shooting everyone on sight out on the streets and dump trucks stacked to capacity with bodies taken to huge burial pits were the normal topic of discussion. Everyone was on edge and it did not help that the gunfire they heard outside was getting more constant as the days went on.

One night, the gunfire never stopped. A young lieutenant came into the gym and pleaded with everyone to remain calm and that the situation was under control. Not long after his speech, the lieutenant and the rest of the soldiers were rushed by several hundred occupants of the gym, who had grown tired of hearing the same reassurances day in and day out. As the soldiers and citizens fought and George could hear the howls of the infected out on the streets, he knew it was time to flee.

He grabbed his partners-Al and Jennifer, the married couple, and Jason, who had grown particularly attached to Jennifer during their time imprisoned there. As most of the refugees ran out onto the streets the foursome moved deeper into the high school. The plan was to get to the back parking lot, away from the soldiers and the infected attackers on the street. Other refugees followed their path but they lost track of everyone else as they roamed the halls of the darkened building. Shots rang out and echoed down the locker filled hallways and George had no idea if it was soldiers firing on the refugees or if the infected had already breached the high school, but had no intention of sticking around to find out.

They finally found their way to the parking lot and that was when they realized they were in as much trouble as the people on the other side of the building.

There were hundreds of plague victims coming through the woods toward the school. They were already in the parking lot and some of the other refugees had made it there before George's quartet. They were struggling to get into the cars crammed in the lot but some were already screaming and being pulled to the ground as the ghouls swarmed them.

"We started running. I'm not quite sure what happened...it gets kind of fuzzy. I just remember seeing those infected people and wondering how they could still be standing. Their guts were hanging out and their arms and legs were missing. I don't really understand it."

George's mouth remained open but he was at a loss for further words. He shook his head several times and Jeff reached over and gripped his shoulder to reassure him that it was okay, that he didn't have to say any more.

George was silent for a while and just as Jeff thought his tale was through, George spoke again, his voice distant and puzzled.

"I'm not really sure how Jason and I made it to that church, how we got back around to the front of the building and crossed the street. I know Al was attacked in the parking lot. Jennifer was trying to help him. I think I was too, but I know that Jason and I ran...I'm just not sure how it all went down." He looked at his hands and turned them so his palms were facing up. "I think I killed someone that night...or maybe it was more than just one. Jason did too...I think we both killed some of those...those..." He was waving his hand, trying to come up with the right word.

"Those *things*?" Jeff interrupted. He leaned forward. "Someone that had been infected?"

George's eyes darted over to Jeff and he put his hands down on top of his cards. He looked confused as he considered what Jeff had said and then nodded slightly.

Jeff shrugged and shook his head. "Then you shouldn't feel all that guilty, George." He shifted in his chair and leaned back. "You did what you had to. I doubt most people in the same situation would have acted differently-at least none that wanted to survive."

"*I* did what I had to, but Jason...," George's eyes widened as he began to remember more details. "I watched him beat one of them to death with some piece of metal he picked up off the ground. He did it without any remorse."

"You say that like it's a bad thing."

George's eyes went wide with surprise. His expression changed and it was hard to see in the moonlight but Jeff could tell that he had struck a nerve.

"Well, you tell me how it can be a good thing that a kid his age...hell, that *anyone* shouldn't give a rip that they just *killed* someone." George's hand slammed down on the table.

Jeff barked out a harsh laugh. He peered into George's eyes to make sure the other man could make out his expression in the dim light. "Reality check, George old pal. Those things are *already* dead. You *can't* kill what's already dead." He leaned back. "Jason and you were just doing those pricks a favor by putting them down for good."

"I'm not so sure about that."

"What!?" Jeff cringed at his own volume. "What?" he repeated, whispering. "Uh, you're not sure those things are already dead or you're not sure you're doing them a favor by putting them out of their misery?"

George stood up and walked across the room, out of the light. "I don't know. Hell, I'm not sure of much of anything anymore."

Jeff shook his head in frustration. "Well George, I *am* sure. Those *things* aren't human anymore. Once I figured that out it got real simple: slaughter them before they slaughter me and maybe I get lucky and live to see another day."

George looked at Jeff from across the room. The younger man's face was pale in the moonlight.

"I'll do what I need to survive and you know that, Jeff. I already have. But that doesn't mean I have to enjoy it. This isn't some sort of game for me."

Jeff's laughter was bitter this time. "So it bugs you that I might be enjoying myself when I take a few of those things out, huh?"

"Yes, yes it does. Self defense is one thing, but enjoying it and killing anyone...or any *thing*, if that's how you prefer to think of it, is a sin."

Jeff waved his hand disdainfully. "Let's not bring God into this."

George looked at Jeff as if he were a child. "How would it be possible, given all that has occurred, not to bring God into this? Or do you think that he has just been sitting on the sidelines this whole time, not paying a bit of attention to what's been going on?"

Jeff held his hands up in a sign of surrender. He was not in the mood for a religious debate, especially with someone who looked raring to go. The apologetic look on his face placated George enough to let it pass. The big man came back to the table and they sat quietly for a few moments, until George, who still had a look of great concentration on his face, spoke up again.

"I don't know, Jeff. I *do* know that murder is a sin. So I'll do what I can to survive and get to my family intact, including defending myself, but I will NOT go out of my way to attack those creatures. You *can't* tell me that you know for certain, without any doubt at all, that there isn't still a spark of humanity left inside them."

"Yes I can."

Jeff had a hard expression on his face, with a tightened jaw and a stern gaze.

"Well, if you're so sure, enlighten me. Please." George spread his hands and waited for an explanation.

Jeff's face darkened and George realized his new found friend was getting angry.

Jeff leaned forward, his eyes flashing with rage. "Have you had to face off against someone you knew, someone who had turned into one of those things?"

The question took George by surprise and he shifted uncomfortably in his chair. He didn't say a word but Jeff already knew his answer.

"Unless you've looked into the eyes of someone you love who's been bitten and turned into one of those things you have *no* idea. Until you look into their eyes and see that there is absolutely *no* recognition or comprehension of who you are anymore, you wouldn't understand."

Jeff continued staring until George had to turn away, uncomfortable with the look in the other man's eyes. Jeff stood up and paced the room.

"I'm sorry Jeff." It was lame, but it was all he had. George didn't look up to see if the other man had acknowledged his apology and heard no response. He looked down at the cards scattered in front of him.

A few minutes later Jeff sat back down across from him, staring out the window. The two sat in silence for a while longer, until it started to become awkward.

"So what happened? If you want to tell me..."

Jeff rubbed his eyes. He looked across at George and felt profoundly exhausted.

There were no sounds except that of the crickets outside, no movement except when a slight breeze moved a branch on one of the trees. Slowly, Jeff began to tell his story.

Chapter 22

Jason was lying in bed on his stomach the next morning when he felt the fingers on his back. He had his pillow wrapped around his head and tried to ignore them as they gently rubbed, coaxing him to get up. He moaned and mumbled something about letting him sleep for just a few more minutes and pulled the pillow tighter.

"Come on Jason, it's time for breakfast." The voice implored. It was muffled and he tried to ignore it, his eyes clenched shut.

"I made your favorite..." The words were soothing, tempting him to get out of the bed. The fingers began scratching his back like he loved.

"Momma, no! I don't wanna get up. Let me sleep for a little while longer," he whined and shook the hand off.

He heard the clicking sound of disapproval and could imagine his mother's head shaking as well, her hands on her hips, like she always did when she started getting irritated with him.

When she pulled his pillow back he shifted onto his back and slowly let his eyes adjust to the morning light.

"Now get up, boy. It's time for my breakfast too."

Jason opened his eyes and saw his mother standing in front of him. She was in the blue scrubs she wore for her job as a nurse in one of the big downtown Cincinnati hospitals. It was splattered with blood. Her tightly braided hair was loose and disheveled, floating around her head. As he looked at her face, he saw that her eyes were cloudy. Her teeth were smashed and blackened as she grinned at him. Bits and pieces of her ashy skin were flaking off.

She touched his face with her hands, which were desiccated and much of the skin was already gone. As she caressed his cheek she began to lean over, her hand slipping behind his neck.

"You better get up now, boy. Cause momma's hungry."

When Jason sat bolt upright he was staring into the startled face of Megan, who had just tapped him lightly on the shoulder.

Megan stumbled back and nearly fell at Jason's reaction. As she clamped her hand to her chest he slid back on his bed toward the wall, his eyes wide with fear.

"Jesus, Jason! You scared the heck out of me!" Megan laughed as her heart pounded fiercely. Shaking her head, she smiled at him.

As she looked on, Megan realized Jason's expression was not gradually relaxing, like hers was. His eyes were still wide with fear as he stared at her and shivered.

"Jason?" The word was hesitant. Megan took a step forward and stopped when the twelve year old scooted further away from her on the bed. "Are you okay, honey?"

Megan gave him a more harmless smile that was bland and non-threatening, but Jason was still backed up against the wall, in the corner of the bed.

A few moments later, as she stood waiting, Jason began to regain his composure. He rubbed his eyes and hid the wetness at their rims.

"I'm okay. Could you just leave me alone, please?" Jason forced the words out slowly to hide any trace of emotion in his voice as he covered his face with his hands. When he pulled them away, Megan was still standing in front of him, the look of concern on her face even greater.

She moved closer to the bed and Jason pressed himself against the wall, shying away like a skittish horse in its pen. Megan hesitated for a moment and then moved forward until she was at the edge of the bed. She sat down at the foot of it, as far from Jason as she could.

"Please don't." Jason said as he scrunched his body up into tight ball.

"Jason, what is it? Please tell me, maybe I can..." He was shaking his head and shivering again. Megan stopped, frozen where she was and said nothing, but continued to stare at him.

The boy wrapped his arms around his legs and buried his face behind them, hiding himself as much as possible from her prying eyes.

"Please go. Just go."

Megan continued to stare at him without moving.

Jason looked over his knees and saw that she was still there, still looking him. "Why haven't you left?! Get out *now!*" His voice was ragged. There was resentment there, but the tremulous anger was a cheap façade covering up something else and Megan saw through it immediately. She knew Jason was afraid of her.

The confusion snapped her out of her frozen state and she crept closer to the boy, unable to stop herself. "No! Get away!" Jason said and looked like he was trying to burrow into the wall. Megan could see the terror on his face as his eyes grew to the size of saucers, as if she was some boogey man or evil troll come to swallow his soul.

She stopped momentarily and stared at him. Jason's face was covered up again behind his knees and his chest was rising and sinking rapidly, as if he was desperately trying to catch his breath. He spoke quietly, whispering between rough sobs and she could barely decipher any of it. "...please no...God please no, no momma no, leave me alone momma please!"

Megan reached out and moved her hand toward the top of his head, hesitating at the last moment. Swallowing hard, she moved her hand down on the boy. He rapidly moved his head back against the wall, a look of terror on his face that curdled her blood.

The look disappeared and Megan tried for a warm smile. It reached her eyes as she moved her hand slowly toward Jason again. His face was filled with dread but he did not try to move away this time.

A single tear rolled down his cheek as the gentle woman's hand touched his face. Jason tensed but did not squirm anymore. She delicately rubbed the tear away and moved her hand across his cheek. He faintly remembered the sensation of the bony fingers caressing him in his nightmare and held back a scream. Megan's fingers felt warm and human though, and the memory began to fade.

"It's okay Jason. I promise it'll be okay," Megan repeated slowly, gently, as he closed his eyes and let her wrap her arms around him. She felt relieved when the twelve year old finally began to relax and his arms slowly slipped around her. When she felt the warmth of his tears on her shoulder she began to rock him and felt her own tears coming in response.

They didn't say anything else as they held one other.

Jeff burst in a few minutes later holding one of the rifles. The woman and the boy jumped apart, startled by the interruption. Jeff did not blink at seeing them comforting one another. He was dressed and the bandages on his head were covered with a baseball cap. He had a tense look on his face.

"It's time to go. Grab everything you can, we're leaving now!"

With that he left. Megan and Jason stared at each other, sheepish smiles crossing their faces.

They were still lost in their own thoughts when they heard a loud thump below. It sounded like it came from outside the house. Before they could react they heard several more loud thuds. A sliver of fear set Megan's hands and feet on pins and needles and she looked at Jason. He looked as frightened as she did. She moved to a window and bent two slats on the blinds to stare out at the front of the house.

Gritting her teeth in anger, she looked out at the wide front yard. There were at least twenty rotting shapes making their way ponderously toward the house.

"How in the hell did they find us already?" Megan cursed.

Several more thumps rattled the outside of the house and they heard glass breaking downstairs.

"Let's move it people! Come on!" Jeff was yelling up the steps as Jason scrambled to pull on a shirt he had found in the dresser. He had slept in his jeans.

"Grab what you can and I'll meet you downstairs!" Megan repeated Jeff's orders and turned to run out the door.

Jason left the room a minute later with a pillow case filled with a few things he had collected from the bedroom. As he hit the stairs, the thunder of a rifle shot made him nearly stumble. He took off toward the kitchen and met George coming the other way.

"Get to the garage, now!" He pushed the boy in front of him as they raced in opposite direction. George was carrying the other rifle and it still looked awkward in his hands.

Another shot rang out from behind them as Megan tore down the steps. George motioned her toward the garage and they sped in that direction.

"Jeff, get to the van now or we're leavin' your ass!" Jason almost laughed when Megan tossed the remark behind her.

They hit the garage and Megan ushered them into the back of the van. George made a half-hearted attempt to get behind the wheel but Megan was having none of it. The keys had been left in the ignition and the engine turned over immediately. Several fists slammed into the wooden garage door in response.

"How in the hell did they find us?" George's question

echoed Megan's earlier inquiry. "I mean, there were none of them around last night. Not a single one. Now there's a whole goddamn platoon? What the hell?"

"They were probably around the area and the noise we made coming here stirred them up. It was only a matter of time before they found us."

"Yeh, but once we got here and settled in, there wasn't much noise for them to pick up on. We don't have any electricity going, we hid the van-"

"I don't know George. No idea." With a shrug of her shoulders Megan dismissed the conversation as she stared at the door leading to the house and squeezed the steering wheel impatiently. Several more fists joined in with the others at the big door behind them and they also began hearing thuds against the plywood they had quickly nailed over the side door window the night before. It would hold, but not for long.

The next minute felt like an eternity as they waited for Jeff. The monotonous thudding was punctuated by another rifle shot inside the house that made everyone jump.

Relief showed on all their faces when the door opened and Jeff ran up to the van. When he heard the big, heavy garage door vibrate behind them he twisted around and pointed the rifle in its direction.

"Come on, get in!" Megan demanded as Jeff swiveled again at hearing other fists slamming into the side door.

"How the hell are we supposed to get out of the garage?" Jeff asked as he kept looking at the different doors, not sure which one was going to break first.

"I'll smash down the door," Megan yelled out at him, exasperation filling her voice.

Jeff shook his head. "You'll do more damage to the van than the door-it's not some cheap aluminum job, its reinforced wood."

Grinding her teeth impatiently, Megan glared at Jeff. "You have a better idea?"

He ignored the sarcasm and looked at the side door

again. He studied it for a moment and Megan saw his face shift and she knew he had come to some sort of a decision. He turned to her and smiled.

"Give me five minutes and then lift the door."

Before she could protest, he was moving quickly over to the side door and unlocking it. Megan's jaw dropped as she watched him.

"Is he insane?" George inquired, horror filling his voice.

She sighed. "George, that's about the only thing I'm certain of anymore."

After a few moments the side door flew open and two rotters burst in, falling forward. Jeff was on them quickly, using the rifle butt to smash in the back of an old man's head. His skin was a dusky grey and the rifle shattered the back of his skull. He toppled over, the force of his landing driving his jaw up into his sinus cavity. All of his bodily fluids had dried up long ago and there was no backsplash of blood or gristle as Jeff finished him off with a swift heel to the back of the head.

The other creature wrapped its hand around one of Jeff's hiking boots. It was probably a woman, its long stringy hair still hanging in clumps from its skull. Leaves and dirt made it impossible to determine her true hair color and weeks out in the elements had burnt most of the exposed skin to a leathery brown. He didn't panic as she lifted her head and dragged herself toward his leg. He whipped around and slammed his other foot on top of her head, pushing it to the ground. He had not used tremendous force, fearing he would topple over with the effort. She continued to struggle, her hands trying to scratch and claw at him.

Jeff shrugged her grasping hand off of his shoe. He maintained his balance and shot a quick look over to the open door. Seeing no one else coming, he put his full weight down on the woman's head. A snap echoed in the garage and he stomped her again. Feeling no more movement underneath his foot, he stepped off the corpse and moved to the door. Peering out, Jeff turned and waved at Megan before moving outside and pulling the door shut behind him.

Megan glanced over at George and back at Jason. They looked as stunned as she felt at Jeff's insane actions.

"I guess all we can do is wait to see if he can pull this one off," she offered weakly and shrugged. They sat and listened as the volume of the moans outside rose as Jeff let out a muffled war cry. Suddenly, the banging on the garage door lessened and they heard sounds of dragging footsteps moving away from it.

Megan listened to Jeff's taunts that mingled with the replies of the infected as he moved further away. She turned to George.

"Okay. Well, the maniac has gotten them away from the door, I guess. I'm going to open it so we can get the hell out of here. George? Can you cover me?" She stared at the big man and saw the nervous look on his face. Sweat was coming off of him in buckets as the rifle sat propped across his legs. His already pale complexion was practically glowing in the semi-darkness of the van's interior. He looked over at her, swallowed hard, and nodded. Megan stared at him for a few more seconds and glanced quickly at Jason. He looked more assured than George. For an instant she was tempted to suggest that he take the rifle but dismissed the idea quickly.

Megan tried to focus on the garage's interior. Lifting the heavy door would only take a second or two then she would be back in the van and safe. It would be easy. She took a deep breath and made the sign of the cross as she pulled on the door handle and slid out of the van.

Moving backwards, she kept one eye on the side door and the two bodies on the floor. They exuded a foul stench that was potent in the enclosed space. George opened the sliding door on the van and pointed the barrel of the rifle toward the door Jeff had left through. Megan turned to examine the garage door's lock.

As she grasped the handle there was a sound of wood shattering behind her and then a loud hissing noise. Megan jumped as a rifle blast echoed through the enclosed room.

Turning, she saw four bodies spilling into the garage from the house. Cursing, she realized that they had forgotten all about the infected chasing Jeff across the interior of the home.

Megan began fumbling for the revolver jammed in her waistband as George stepped out of the van and lined up another shot. She tugged at the gun as the second blast rang out. She was struggling with the .357's hammer, which was snagged on her shirt.

Wrestling it free, she moved next to George. All four rotters were still closing in and she aimed at the closest.

A puff of smoke came out of the barrel as the bullet punched a hole in its chest. A spray of black mist came out its back and drenched the next stiff in line. Though stumbling slightly, it kept moving forward. Megan saw its mouth move but the ringing in her ears blotted out its howl of rage.

George awkwardly rammed another cartridge in place on the bolt action rifle and fired his third shot. Megan saw a puff of dust as the bullet went wild, striking drywall two feet from any of the targets.

"Get the bat!" She screamed as she tried to steady her hand and take aim once again.

Her next shot passed through the upper cheek of her closest enemy, which was less than ten feet in front of her. It moved a half step forward as its head rocked backwards and then it folded up like a lawn chair as it landed on its back. The others were unfazed and continued coming. Megan took a breath and fired at the next, puckering its nasal cavity. A dangling piece of cartilage broke free from its nose as the body crumpled to the cement.

The last two were almost on top of her. Fighting rising panic and her shaking hands, the next shot was off mark, blowing a hole in the third monster's shoulder. Its arms were extended, reaching for her and the fourth was beside it, ready to pull her down.

Megan could finally hear their excited moans as they got close. Eyes wide, she took aim as a clammy hand gripped her arm. She felt the dry, cold skin as the bony fingers wrapped tightly around her elbow, yanking the weapon off target.

Pulling the trigger, she felt a bolt of pain that was a combination of the recoil and the sensation of her arm being nearly yanked out of its socket. Suddenly, hands that had been reaching for Megan's neck fell away and there was a white hot burst of pain as she was knocked to the ground.

Tumbling sideways, she could feel the cold grip on her arm release as she was slammed to the garage floor. Doing her best to ignore the pain flaring through her shoulder, she rolled over and tried to raise the gun again.

As things came into focus she saw George slamming the last of the infected up against the garage wall. Megan tried to take aim but George was already charging at it like a lineman, a bellow of rage bursting free from his lips.

He connected, driving the monster into the drywall and creating a crater in it. George quickly backed up a few feet but continued bellowing taunts at the obscenity slumped before him.

Megan did not blink as she watched the madman encourage the rather rotund rotter to pull itself out of the new wall niche and stagger toward him. The first kick connected with its chest, driving it back into the hole. The second drove it toward the ground, where George unleashed a flurry of blows to its head while it tried to grab at him. It obsessively scratched and pawed at the man looming above it until Megan heard a distinctive *pop* and saw its arms convulse slightly and flop to the ground. George stomped on its head a few more times for good measure.

The battle over, he leaned against the wall above his handiwork, panting heavily. Megan let her hand holding the gun drop to her lap as she took a deep breath herself. The other stiff, the one George had pulled off of her, lay nearby, its neck bent awkwardly from where it had been brutally snapped.

A moment later her guardian was looming over Megan, his arm extended. He no longer looked frightened, as he did when he was wielding the rifle. His jaw was set and she could see the determined look in his eyes.

"Let's get the hell out of here."

Megan nodded and took his hand. George pulled her up like she weighed nothing. She looked in the van and saw Jason in the doorway, staring out at them. The rifle George had discarded was in his hands and his eyes held a tinge of fear.

Megan gave him a wink and Jason responded with a nervous smile. She stuffed the revolver into her pants and moved toward the garage door. George stood watch, tensed for more action as he peered through the shattered doorway leading into the house.

She pressed her ear to the wood and listened. There was a great deal of moaning but none of it nearby as far as she could tell. Jeff apparently was still keeping the infected at bay. As Megan leaned down to pull the heavy door up by its handle, she was certain that sooner or later one of his crazy stunts was going to end up getting him killed.

"If he isn't dead already," she mumbled under her breath.

Jeff spotted the van after it pulled out of the garage. Megan spun the wheel in a one-eighty so it faced the road and caught sight of him as he waved her forward. The infected were all over the yard, most falling all over one another in an effort to close on him as he pranced around and taunted them. He had taken the occasional pot shot with the rifle but the yard was a wide expanse and had given him plenty of room to maneuver and avoid the infected's threatening embrace.

Megan drove in his direction, knocking aside a few stiff bodies attracted by the growling engine. As she drew closer Jeff waved again, relief painted on his face.

The van skidded to a halt on the grass and the sliding door opened. Jeff ran for it and George's beefy arm shot out and grabbed a hold of his shirt and yanked him in. Megan floored it and they shot down the gravel drive, spraying rocks and dust behind them.

Jeff let out a cheer and pumped his fist as George glared at him. "Whoo hoo! We made it!" He shouted and laughed wildly.

"You're fucking nuts! Do you know that?" George said as he shook his head.

Jeff laughed some more as he took several deep breaths. His face was red with exhaustion but he felt invigorated.

"Yep, but I'm still alive," he said as he slapped George on the back. "We're *all* still alive!"

George just gave him another sour look as he leaned back in his chair and crossed his arms.

Megan pulled them out onto the road and her eyes widened as she saw how many of ghouls were stomping through the cornfields, moving toward the house. Jeff slid into the passenger seat beside her, the grin still on his face. When he looked up and saw the crowd of stiffened bodies, his smile faltered slightly.

"This is never going to end, is it?" She asked quietly.

Jeff stared at a boy in a pair of overalls hobbling toward the van, his stiff legs betraying him as it passed. As he tumbled to the ground he raised his arm up again, still reaching for them.

As Jeff settled into his seat he had no answer for Megan. His smile faded as he let his head touch the window. He didn't say a word as the endless rows of corn flew by.

Chapter 23

Megan drove slowly down the road and stared out at the flat expanse ahead.

The debate over where to go had been short and she had been in the minority. Manchester was the logical choice for them to find George a car and other survivors. Even after having lived through Milfield and Gallatin Jeff was the biggest proponent of checking out the town.

As she glanced off into the distance she would see the occasional stiff body moving in their direction but none close to the road. Many of the buildings and houses looked normal. It took a discerning eye to see the occasional broken window, door hanging ajar, or a splash of blood on a sidewalk that broke up the monotony.

As they rolled on there were no abrupt changes to the landscape but it was clear they were getting close to Manchester. The houses, previously spread out, were starting to bunch up again. The telephone poles, always a constant alongside the road, were becoming more prolific.

A speed limit sign told them they needed to slow down to forty five. It was an indication that they were getting close to the town. Beyond the sign were several abandoned vehicles that had been tossed around like matchbox cars. None were in good shape and many were turned on their sides or flipped entirely.

Up ahead the road curved out of sight. Before that it

narrowed slightly, a train bridge running across it. A bright yellow sign hung on the overpass indicating that no vehicles over 13' 11" could pass underneath. The cheery note stood out against a drab brown backdrop of rusted metal. Megan stared at the opening apprehensively as they moved closer.

There were no vehicles blocking their passage but there was a pickup truck that had slammed into the guard rail. The back of the Tundra was still peaking out of the ditch on the right side of the road.

"Here we go. Manchester straight ahead." Jeff said as he peered out the windshield.

George was behind Megan and she could almost feel his breath on her neck as he gawked at the damaged vehicles. She heard a grunt of frustration as he saw that none were in driving condition.

As they moved under the bridge and on to the other side nothing in the scenery changed. The van glided around a curve in the road that moved them southeast. Four sets of eyes scanning the immediate area for signs of activity saw none. There were no indications of military presence: no barricades, no razor wire, and no corpses.

The road continued to serpentine, now to the north as they moved closer to Manchester. To the left they saw a plain, squared off cinder block building that looked like a bomb had gone off in it. A huge gaping hole on its front allowed them to see that the inside looked as bad as the exterior. There was a ragged stump of a lamp post in the parking lot and the broken metal shaft was lying on the street. It had snapped in several places and was spread across the roadway. The cement base was still intact and the metal shards sprouting out of it vomited corroded wires. Only the free standing awning over four gas pumps and a darkened outline of the letters M-A-R-T on the side of the structure gave any hint as to what purpose the building had once served.

A road cut north before the gas station. A sign, badly damaged, pointed travelers down the path but it was hard to tell what the name of the road was. The sign was bent sideways and caked with layers of clay or mud. As Megan looked closer her stomach roiled. Some of the mud on the sign was rather ropy and viscous.

"That's Route One Twenty Three." Megan glanced over at Jeff, glad for the distraction of his voice as he pointed at the road in question. "It splits to the north here but merges with the main drag ahead of us. We'll have to go a bit further into town and then maybe we can turn south."

That had been the plan. They would find a car for George, wish him luck, and then find some road that wasn't clogged up which would hopefully lead them further from more clots of infected population.

Megan slowed the van and scanned the gas station. Nothing stirred inside as they rolled along. Beyond it the roadway looked almost normal, like it would in any sleepy Midwestern town. She gave the building another glance as they slowly passed and noticed more signs facing away from them on the left side of the road. As they went by she glanced at them. One welcomed drivers to Harris Township while another informed them they were entering Warren and leaving Clinton County. The other two narrow green signs gave distance markings to towns that were north on Route 123.

George tightened his grip on the back of Megan's chair as he stared at the last two signs. The words on them were: *Morris-10* and *Liston-19.*

He felt a hand on his shoulder and his eyes darted over to Jeff. "How far is Wildwood from here?"

George looked back at the sign again, his eyes distant as he thought about the question. "Thirty, maybe thirty five miles north."

Jeff grunted his acknowledgement before turning to stare out the window again.

There were more buildings on both sides of the street past the convenience store. They were widely spaced with ample grassy areas between them. Gravel topped parking lots were shared by simple, drab tin buildings. There were no streets behind the businesses, just farmland...flat open fields interspersed with small wooded areas. The buildings looked tired and worn down. They consisted of faded paint and dirty facades with some looking like they had been abandoned long ago. There were a few boarded up windows and others were shattered, but it looked like this part of Manchester had been a ghost town long before the infected had come. A couple of small billboards for McDonalds and a new subdivision from Vancouver Builders (*Homes starting in the $120's*) were ripped and tattered but did their best to dispute the image of a town that had been slowly dying for years. The buildings that stretched along the road made out of wood and corrugated tin looked dated. "Scrubbing Bubbles" Car Wash and Laundromat, Cockrell's Family Dining, and a Bridgestone Tire Store were just a few of the businesses that welcomed the foursome to the remains of Manchester.

The unnatural stillness outside was a good match for the silence inside the van. Even the engine noise of the Odyssey only had the chirping of a few birds and insects as competition.

The road began to straighten out and they were now moving southeast. They began to see cars and trucks lined up on both sides of the road in front of even more commercial structures. Some were parked normally while others looked like they had been pushed aside by something huge.

Looking ahead toward the crowd of vehicles, Jeff assessed the situation. "Well George, we should be able to find you a car in no time."

Jeff was hunched over, rifle in hand as he stared ahead, looking inside each vehicle for signs of movement. There wasn't any and he glanced over at yet another sign that dotted the entrance of the town. It was tattooed with emblems of all the civic organizations that had chapters in Manchester: the Rotarians, the Jaycees, etc. A few of the churches had also joined in with placards encouraging folks to attend the Church of Christ or United Methodist. Like everything else in the town, the sign had seen better days and leaned precipitously to one side. A message in the bottom right hand corner stated the sign was courtesy of McDonalds.

Still, he saw no bodies, living or dead, anywhere. Jeff could feel the sweat rising up on his brow as he searched the area once again for movement.

Near the wooden sign and closer to the van were more buildings. There was a sizeable gap between two of the drab one story structures he was staring at. Railroad tracks ran behind it with farmland even further back. Jeff spied a house off in the distance about a half of a mile away and some dense woodland beyond. Nothing moved as he looked at the landscape carefully.

On the opposite side of the road several businesses crowded close to the street for a stretch. More billboards vied for attention along with a bright yellow Dollar General sign close to the road. Small parking lots that were mostly empty provided a gap between the road and darkened buildings. On the other side the nondescript boxy brown shops were even closer to the road, no further back than ten or fifteen feet. A row of vehicles served as a buffer between them and the van.

They started moving between the two lines of cars which appeared to stretch about a quarter of a mile down the straight-away. The path between them was tight but gave the van enough room to maneuver. At the beginning of the line a car was angled sideways on the right side of the road. Jeff stared down at it and nodded to himself.

"Let's check out all of these cars, but I think that first one might be your best bet." He gestured with his head as George looked out the window to examine the vehicle.

His eyes grew wide as they drove past the car. It looked good and so did several others. Megan and Jeff were studying them as well and didn't notice Jason peering out the rear of the van, or even when he moved back to the third row of seats.

"Guys, I think you better look behind us."

The van slowed as everyone turned to look at whatever it was that had caught the boy's eye.

Jason had not been too concerned about finding George a car to get home. The close encounters he had with both the infected and the living over the past few days had him on edge. So when he saw the shadow shift near one of the cars he immediately assumed it was a ghoul. When a head popped up from behind the vehicle, and whoever it was started running, he did a double take. It certainly didn't look like one of the infected.

"What the-?"

Jeff moved next to Jason, wading past the seats and piles of supplies they had collected. When he looked out the window he could not believe what he was seeing.

The van came to a stop as Megan turned to see what was up. Now George was in the back as well and the three were blocking her view.

"Well, what is it?"

One of the cars was moving. The very first one they had seen. The one that had been perpendicular to the others. It had quietly rolled into the middle of the road. Jeff and George shared a glance, confusion etched on their faces.

It was Jeff who realized what was happening first and turned to face Megan, whose look of exasperation at a lack of explanation quickly changed. "Get out of here! Now!"

Megan swallowed another question as she turned around. Her foot moved to the gas but before she could touch it, her eyes widened at what she was seeing out the windshield.

It was already too late.

While they had been busy studying what was going on behind them another car had pulled onto the road up front, at the end of the quarter mile long stretch of vehicles. They were cut off.

Megan saw a figure pop up over the hood of a Nissan Maxima nearby. It was holding a semi-automatic pistol pointed directly at her head. Someone else holding a rifle was behind a Volvo station wagon on the other side of the street.

Jeff rushed back to the front of the van just in time to see another man popping up between the cars outside. Freezing between the seats, Jeff's breathing grew harsh. He spied Megan out of the corner of his eye and saw that she had gone rigid as well. In that moment he wished he could turn invisible as he saw the man outside taking aim at him with an M16.

"Shit, there are two guys pointing shotguns at us!"

When George heard no response to his comment he turned and saw that Jeff was not moving. Jason was bent over in his seat, his hands covering his head. Most importantly, in George's mind, was the fact that they were not flying down the road to escape the impending attack from behind.

"You, in the van. Show your hands, *now!* Make a move toward any weapons and we start shooting!"

Fear sliced through the four survivor's minds like a razor as they heard the voice shouting from outside. Slowly, Jeff, Megan, and George began raising their hands. Jason, realizing they were not going to be shot at (at least not immediately) sat up carefully and slowly raised his hands as well as he stared out the back window.

As the men outside inched closer to the minivan, Jeff's mind raced over the events of the last few days. He had not cared whether he lived or died when he fled his house but there were others relying on him now and he had more than enough reasons to want to stay alive.

But as he stared down the barrel of a rifle for the second time in as many days, he was beginning to doubt he was going to last much longer.

About the Author

Patrick D'Orazio resides in southwestern Ohio with his wife, Michele, two children, Alexandra and Zachary, and three spastic dogs. He has been writing since he was a teenager but only recently clued into the fact that unless he attempted to get published, no one else would really care.

Several of his short stories appear in various anthologies from Library of the Living Dead, including "The Moron's Guide to the Inevitable Zombocalypse," "The Zombist," "Night of the Giving Dead," "Zombidays," and "Letters from the Dead." He will also be appearing in May December's "Eyewitness: Zombie" anthology and Pill Hill Press' "Daily Bites of Flesh 2011."

Comes The Dark, the first book of a trilogy, is Patrick's first novel.

You can find Patrick on his Facebook Page (Patrick D'Orazio), or at his blog (www.patrickdorazio.com) or kicking around on the boards of The Library of the Living Dead (www.libraryofthelivingdead.lefora.com).

Made in the USA
Lexington, KY
20 March 2011